SIXSHOOTER

BOOKS BY DEAN F. WILSON

THE CHILDREN OF TELM

The Call of Agon
The Road to Rebirth
The Chains of War

THE GREAT IRON WAR

Hopebreaker
Lifemaker
Skyshaker
Landquaker
Worldwaker
Hometaker

THE COILHUNTER CHRONICLES

Coilhunter
Rustkiller
Dustrunner
Lostlander
Sixshooter
Deadwalker

HIBERNIAN HOLLOWS

Hibernian Blood
Hibernian Charm

A COILHUNTER CHRONICLES NOVEL

SIXSHOOTER

DEAN F. WILSON

Cover illustration by Duy Phan

First Edition 2021

ISBN 978-1-909356-31-3

DIOSCURI PRESS

Published by Dioscuri Press
Dublin, Ireland

www.dioscuripress.com
enquiries@dioscuripress.com

Welcome to the Wild North

CONTENTS

1	The Noose	09
2	Blame	13
3	Catch	16
4	Guns for Grains	20
5	A Warm Welcome	23
6	The Farmlands	26
7	Vengeance	32
8	Protection	38
9	Desert Driveby	42
10	The Dawn of War	45
11	The Hand and the Eye	49
12	The Slaughter Streets	52
13	Slaughterer Nox	55
14	The Battle of the Burg	59
15	A Thousand Names to Kill	67
16	The Devil of the Deadmakers	70
17	The Forever Barflies	74
18	Meeting at Midnight	79
19	The High Valleys	83
20	The Dew Monster	90
21	Pulleytown	95
22	A Forbidden Love	101
23	Men in the Mines	103
24	The Monsters in Men	108
25	A War of Wire and Lead	113
26	The Powder Kegs	119
27	The Bang	121
28	The Train or the Tracks	127
29	The Ironking	131

Chapter

30	Double or Nothing	136
31	Handcart Ranch	141
32	Robbers and Rifles	145
33	Not So Shy	150
34	Overrun	153
35	Three Wheels, Two Engines	155
36	That Multi-Coloured Cavalry	158
37	Hell in a Handbasket	161
38	The War on Wheels	164
39	The Butcher of the Bikers	169
40	When the Dust Settles	176
41	Just Paper and Charcoal	179
42	Catchin' Up	183
43	Right in a Row	187
44	Buryin' the Hatchet	190
45	Tombthief	193
46	The Tree of Life	197
47	One For Each of You	201
48	Better Terms	206
49	That Temporary Peace	211

Chapter One

THE NOOSE

It started with six. Six people. Six bodies. Six families waiting for their loved ones to come home, and kept forever waiting.

Nox watched them for a moment, hanging from one of the many outcroppings that dotted the landscape, when the desert dared to cough up any features at all. They hung by the neck, like criminals. And maybe some of them were. But not all of them. Or not by choice. There were kids up there, three of them. Sure, the gangs got them young. But it looked like the other gangs got them younger. That wasn't the way of things, but the Wild North had a way of showing you every day that there could be a new, more wretched way.

It was wrong, but then the Wild North revelled in wrong. Any other night, Nox wouldn't have batted a dust-covered eyelid. Not because he didn't care. But because he couldn't care for them all, for all the dead and the dying, the slaves and the sand-parched free.

But this night, it got to him more than most. Maybe it was how young they were. One must've been no more than five years old, about the age of his own little Aaron when he was snatched from the world.

Nox had made many silent promises, but more than anything he promised to get the snatchers. He'd spent his lifetime hunting them. He'd spent their lifetimes with a spinning barrel.

Nox had many names in the Wild North. The Coilhunter. The Rustkiller. The Lawlasher. Yet here these six bodies were, dead with no names. That whole damn rock feature was their unmarked tombstone. Something in Nox told him that it was big enough to house some more.

"This is gonna start a war," a voice came from behind him.

Nox was so caught up in his thoughts he'd lost his surroundings. You didn't do that too many times in the Wild North or you ended up with a noose of your own, if you were allowed to even keep your head. Yet his instincts already had him sling his pistol towards the phantom voice.

"Easy now," the woman said. She was old and worn, like the desert wears the young. Her features had just as much erosion as the granite arch. Yet there she stood, leaning heavy on a walking stick, while the young hung from the desert's rafters. In the Wild North, the Devil tried to lasso you from your feet, but God hung you from above.

"Easier if you tell me who you are," the Coilhunter rasped. A ceremonial puff of black smoke fired from his mask, like a warning shot. He needed that mask to breathe, and it connected to the chemical tanks on his back, his constant physical burden. There was another one too, an almost spiritual one, that he carried. It was the weight of a world that'd given up, letting the criminals run rampant, letting the conmen roam free.

"Agatha," the woman croaked. She had her own grit, but, unlike Nox, it didn't make her sound sinister. "Agatha Cotten."

"Like the Scorpion? Like Taberah?"

"Only in name, dear. There ain't no one out there like her."

"She said you were dead."

"Dead to her, yes. I didn't go in for her war, y'see."

"The Great Iron War," Nox mused. That'd been raging for years down south, and east, and west. Everywhere bar the Wild North. The desert rolled on in all directions, but up here it had a will of its own. Some called it a sleeping god. Some called it a timeless spirit. Nox called it an enemy. If he could've hauled a large enough Wanted poster out, he would've painted on the face of the desert and got to work. The Wild North must've known it, because it gave him plenty of other work with its inhabitants to do first.

"And this," Agatha said, pointing a finger towards the noose-tied six, yet never lifting her hand from her walking stick. "Well, this'll start another."

"That's the last thing we need."

"Maybe not the last, if you've got any imagination, Coilhunter, but we're gettin' it all the same."

"I assume they're known," Nox said. "In the gangs, I mean."

"Known, sure," Agatha said. "And loved. That's the dangerous part."

Nox almost humphed. "Is love dangerous?"

"Depends who you love, dear."

Nox didn't have an answer for that. He knew all

too well that anyone who loved him was in danger. His wife and kids had learned that. Maybe others would too, if he'd ever let them in. That's why he had to fight alone. That's why, when the time came, he'd have to die alone too.

"Tell me," Nox said, and his eyes told her to tell him quick. "Who did this?"

"You did, Coilhunter," the woman said. "You did."

Chapter Two

BLAME

Nox had been blamed for many things over the years. He was the Man of a Thousand Names, after all. Some of those names were associated, rightly or wrongly, with some questionable deeds. If you were there at the crime scene, you just pasted your own Wanted poster to the wall. Nox'd learned that all too well when the Wild North's opportunistic bounty hunters turned on him before. But this was different. This time, the blame was kind of true, in its own roundabout way, in the way the dominoes topple. Well, Nox'd toppled quite a few.

"Tell me," Nox drawled. "How'd I do this, huh?"

"You did it when you killed Lawless Lyle," Agatha told him. "You did it when you removed the one man the others feared, the one keepin' the peace."

"He was no peacekeeper," Nox said. "He was a monster."

"That he was. But he was *our* monster, and they feared him because of it. Now there are many monsters."

"There were always many."

"Well, they hadn't all come out of the darkness before."

"Let 'em come," Nox said. "It's time they see the light."

"Oh, they'll come. This feud between the Silent Sickles and the Good Gullet Gang goes back almost a generation, back before the Iron Empire came. It was tit-for-tat for years, until Lawless Lyle got 'em to agree a truce, in that ever so convincin' way he had."

"And now he's gone."

Agatha sighed. "And now he's gone."

"So, who are these then?" Nox gestured towards the dangling bodies without turning 'round. He'd already seen their blank stares. He didn't need to see them again.

"The youngest, the boy, is the child of Frank Five-eyes."

"The leader of the Silent Sickles," Nox mused.

"Always watchful, always careful," Agatha said. "They say he has those two eyes at the front, one on the back, one on either side, and one above."

"Spies, you mean."

"If you call 'em that, sure."

"Well, he didn't see this comin', now, did he?"

"He did, in a way. He was long against any move that might upset the stability of the Wild North, unlike his father."

"Stability." Nox humphed. "There ain't no stability here."

"Oh, but there is. Maybe it's the stability of many rocks precariously balanced on each other, standin' against the sand and the wind, yet ever so easy to topple."

"They needed to topple."

"Perhaps, but Frank Five-eyes didn't see it that way."

"And what about now? What about with his kid strung up?"

"He might see it a little differently."

"And the others? Who are they?"

"Relatives of the Free Farmlords. Five different families."

"Under the protection of the Silent Sickles," Nox said.

"So, what would you do, Coilhunter, if they took your young?"

Nox let out his sigh long and slow. They already had, all those years ago. His boy and girl. Little Aaron and Ambrose. He'd gone for vengeance, and though he'd kind of gotten it, he was still seeking it in his own way, punishing every wrongdoer as if they were the ones who'd done that particular wrong. He didn't think he'd ever stop hunting, and just hoped he'd be buried with his gun. Folk said you should only fear the living. Well, Nox said you'd fear him, alive or dead.

"They'll want vengeance," the Coilhunter rasped.

Agatha nodded. "They'll want blood."

And there, right on cue, like the unseen finger of a god prodding the next great domino, came a gunshot from the dunes. They wanted blood. They all did. And the Wild North always delivered.

Chapter Three

CATCH

"Get down!" Nox shouted, as the bullets pelted the sand around them. Agatha fell to the ground as the Coilhunter charged towards his vehicle, a large monowheel parked nearby, with one large tank-treaded wheel around a seat and an engine, with a box for bounties in the back. He leapt into the driver seat and fired it up, zooming up one of the dunes.

Night, like day, conspired against him, cloaking the gunners. They said night fell darker in the Wild North to better hide the criminals. They said the glare of the daylight sun did the same. None of it mattered to the Coilhunter. God himself could've shielded them, and he'd still get in that winning shot.

He bashed his fist on his wristpad. In the dark skies above there was a sound of mechanical wings and the hooting of an owl. Moments later, in the dark dunes that disguised the shooters, two spotlights blared down, searching out the culprits.

Nox's monowheel thundered up the dunes, following the movement of the owl as it caught a scrambling figure in its glare. The engine rumbled with its own machine anger, and the exhaust at the back blasted out its thick black smoke to match the

Coilhunter's mask.

He saw the figure darting in and out of the spotlight, slipping down a steeper ridge. Nox leapt out of his seat without even stopping the vehicle, letting it roll on ahead as he charged after the gunman. He spotted the man's fallen pistol in the sand and yanked it up with one hand while firing a grapnel from the launcher on his other arm. He reeled the frantic figure in with a tap on his wristpad, and boy did he squirm like a fish. Catch of the day. No, catch of the night.

"Oh God," the man cried.

"I ain't your god," the Coilhunter boomed, and he said it like the Devil.

"Please," the gunner begged.

"Oh, *now* you've found your manners. There's a code to a gunfight, boy, and it starts with an introduction. You don't go gunnin' from the hills. You let 'em know who ya are first. You let 'em know your name."

The man was whimpering now, barely able to say anything at all. When he glanced up through his tear-covered eyes, he saw the silhouette that haunted the nightmares of all criminals in the Wild North, and thought of all the stories, all the legends—and feared that they were true.

"No name, huh?" Nox said. "Guess it'll be an unmarked grave then."

"It was just a job."

"No. It was more than that. It was a life. Or many. Maybe mine. Maybe hers. Maybe those poor six hangin' high in the sky." He'd spotted the rope on the man's waist, and the rope burns on his hands.

He'd certainly done some hanging that night. "Or, ya know, maybe yours."

"I had to. I had to hang 'em. You can't kill me for doin' my job!"

"Well, you can't stop me from doin' mine."

And the Coilhunter did it with the gunman's gun. All it took was a single round, right between the eyes. They say the eyes were the window to the soul. Well, you couldn't just kill the man then. You had to get him all. You could cash in the body to Logan Hardwell at the Bounty Booth, or whoever was the latest appointment by the Iron Empire. And the soul? Well, maybe there was a Bounty Booth in Heaven. You could bet lucky there was one in Hell.

Nox didn't loiter. A low-pitched beep on his wristpad told him that the owl had found another one. It seemed that no matter how many posters Nox ripped down, there was always room for more. The driverless monowheel followed the flight of the owl, chasing down the second gunman. When Nox caught up, he found the man pinned to the ground beneath the metal treads of the vehicle. The owl flapped fiercely above.

"Hidin' in the dark, huh?"

The spotlight glare from the mechanical owl above drew out every detail. Oh, there was rope on his waist too, and those same incriminating marks on his hands.

"You should've known I'd find ya."

"Please, Coilhunter."

"You should've known I'd kill ya."

"I only held the rope."

"Well, I only hold this gun."

"It was payback."

"And who's now gonna pay you?"

"I was under orders!"

"Well, here's an order," the Coilhunter croaked. "Go to Hell."

He unloaded two bullets this time, clean and cold, unlike the chaotic gunfire of the gunners before. Of course, the problem with telling someone to go to Hell in the red sands of Altadas was that they could pretty rightfully reply: *Oh, we're already there.* Nox'd thought he'd gotten the Devil. They called him Lawless Lyle. But, you see, Hell has many devils. Well then, Nox'd have to get them all.

Chapter Four

GUNS FOR GRAINS

Nox returned to Agatha, with those two bodies in the box at the back of the monowheel. He leapt out when he saw the old woman on the ground, clutching her side.

"They got ya, huh?"

"Blood for blood," Agatha coughed.

"But you're not their enemy."

"Does it matter, dear? This is how it goes. The war takes us all."

"You'll live," Nox said. He rarely ever said that. He certainly didn't say it to the criminals.

"For a while, perhaps. Can you get me to the Farmlands? Maybe there they can give me a proper burial."

Nox didn't nod or agree, in case the fates saw him agreeing to her burial. He bundled Agatha into the box at the back, where it was already cramped. Some called it "the temporary coffin," as more often than not when you sat in there, you were already dead. That didn't bode well for Agatha.

The journey towards the Farmlands used up the remaining hours of the night. The monowheel cut through the sand as the headlights cut through the darkness. The featureless expanse dropped away in shadow, until here and there the silhouettes of trees appeared, and finally the sandy carpet gave way to cracked earth and parched grasses. You had to go far north for that, to tribal territory, though some of that land had been taken by the Silent Sickles. They called it the Farmlands, but it wasn't just farms. It was a fortress.

"Guns for grains," Nox muttered to himself as the vast walls appeared on the horizon. There were ruins of castles in some parts of Altadas, but they were nothing like this. Those walls were impenetrable, or so they said, and there were artillery dotted across the ramparts. In a world of desert, you defended every last patch of green earth. It was just a pity the criminals were the ones defending it.

Nox stopped short of the artillery range and hauled Agatha to her feet.

"We'll need to walk the rest," he said. "You'll need to tell 'em not to fire."

"Oh, don't you worry, Coilhunter."

"I'll stop worryin' when this war's over, and the one down south as well."

Agatha hobbled along the road towards the vast gate. She produced a flag from her pocket, bearing the symbol of three interwoven blades of corn and waved it from hip to high heavens. Nox couldn't hear the clink of the artillery adjustments from his distance, but he saw them pointing at her now.

"You are on Farmlands territory," a voice boomed out over a loudspeaker. "Declare your allegiance."

Agatha produced a second flag, this one bearing

two sickles, one upright and one reverse, to form the letter S, the emblem of the Silent Sickles Gang. She waved this too, though less vigorously. It was unclear if this was because she was less loyal to them or increasingly less loyal to life. The blood splatters around her painted their own answer. Nox just hoped she wouldn't have to wave a white flag to Death as well.

The gate opened slightly, enough to let out a truck armed with machine guns. It trundled up to her and halted mere inches away, with all guns pointed at her. Armed men jumped off the back of the truck and patted Agatha down violently. They shouted questions at her, and she answered them all in detail, revealing what'd happened that night. They didn't seem content with her answers. Perhaps that was because they knew the implications of them.

If that's how you greet a friend, Nox thought, *then what about an enemy?*

That's when they spotted him, standing beside his monowheel farther back.

Well, let's find out.

Chapter Five

A WARM WELCOME

The alarms blared and the spotlights came on, pinpointing the Coilhunter in their glare. It was broad daylight, but the shadow of the walls had hidden Nox before. He stood there for a moment, hands raised, until he saw the silhouette of machine guns on the ramparts, shifting their aim towards him.

Now, in the Wild North you had a choice: you could keep your hands up and hope the other man didn't shoot you anyway, or you could assume he'd already fired and get in a shot of your own. Hope was a drug in Altadas, an enemy. And in the Wild North so was just about everything else. So Nox didn't wait with his hands up. He dived into the shadow to the side just seconds before the bullets came.

The spotlights chased him, but at this point they were just chasing shadows in the smoke he'd already spread along his path. The gunners killed the sand and punched a few holes in the monowheel's tank, letting the diesel spill out, but it beat punching holes in him and letting the blood spill out instead.

As he ran, he dropped a larger canister from his back, just beneath his oxygen tanks. As soon as it landed, it sprang open, erecting a scarecrow version of the Coilhunter, hat and all, in a matter of seconds. It wasn't much to look at up close, but from afar you would've sworn it was Nox himself, staring out of the haze.

The gunners targeted the decoy, allowing Nox to slip up close to the wall, out of their line of sight. He launched a grapnel to the top and hoisted himself up, before knocking out one of the gunners with the back of his own gun. By rights he should've killed the man. But that was the thing. It was rights that stopped him. That funny old notion that you deserved to live until you did something against life itself. The gangs didn't get that. That's why they had this feud. That's why they'd have this war.

If Nox wanted to, he could've fought his way across the ramparts, taking out every gunner along the way. But he wasn't there to fight. He was no warrior. He was there to stop a war, to stop the Farmlords and the Silent Sickles from looking for revenge. Maybe he had no right to do that, given his own past quest for vengeance, but there was a difference between righting one wrong and making several others. Most said the Wild North didn't have any laws, so someone had to make them. Most said the Wild North didn't have a sheriff, so someone had to don the badge.

He turned the gun and pointed it into the central plaza, where there were many of the Farmlords' "high society" languishing on bed-chairs in the sun, while the farmers toiled in the endless fields behind them. Nox turned on the spotlight to give them a little extra burn.

"You said *howdy* with lead," Nox shouted down.

"Let me say it back."

Some of the ganglords tried to flee, but others held them back, wanting to give the Coilhunter no excuse to gun them down. General Rommond of the Resistance had a saying: *If you walk these sands, you run the risk of making it a grave as well as a home.* Nox could think of his own: *If you run, you gotta ask yourself who you're runnin' from. And if you need an answer, I'll give ya one: It'll be me.*

Chapter Six

THE FARMLANDS

Oh, those Farmlords didn't bask for long before the sweat was visible. They stared up at the glare of the spotlight, seeing just the shadow of the Coilhunter behind—that same shadow that stalked the nightmares of all the conmen and criminals. Nox kept the gun on them, even though he knew they kept the others on him.

A well-fed man with well-fed whiskers took off his sun hat and waved it at the Coilhunter. He cleared his throat noisily and held the hat to his chest as he talked. He was all in white, and that included his hair and his moustache, but also his clothes. They didn't have a spot on them from the fields.

"My apologies, Coilhunter," the man shouted up, "but we don't see your type around these parts, and let's just say everyone's on edge since Lawless Lyle's passin'. A welcome with guns ain't what anybody wants, but with your reputation you're lucky you get a welcome at all."

"I could say the same about you, Baron." Nox knew he was the Baron, not because of how he dressed or spoke, but because he dared to speak at all. He was of the old nobility that'd since become the Treasury, but he'd fled up north with some of their fortune. He was Baron Brooks, one of the Farmlords, and he wasn't just a mouth—he was the one with power too.

"You could, and maybe you do," the Baron said, "but there ain't no poster with my face on it, and we all know you follow a code of sorts. So do we. Of sorts."

"*Of sorts* is stretchin' it for you."

"In the Wild North, you gotta stretch everything, Nox. Hell, you gotta stretch life itself." He wasn't wrong there, but the Coilhunter preferred the criminals to do a stretch of their own. Either in prison, or a little bit longer in that prison underground.

"Here, let me get a better look at you." The Baron approached closer and took out a monocle. He eyed the Coilhunter up and down. "Uhm, uhm, uhm. The Coilhunter in the flesh. Well, ain't that a sight for sore eyes."

"I can make 'em sorer," Nox replied.

The Baron laughed boisterously. "Gotta love ya if we didn't hate ya so much."

"I've got no time for love."

"More's the pity, Coilhunter. Or should I call you somethin' different? Somethin' new? Sure, ain't I even got a visitor book in my quarters with a few dozen of your names. Not that you ever visit. But we've gotta have you down in the blacklist, don't we? Or shall I add in another name?"

"You can add it in blood," Nox said. "Here, let me help ya." He shifted slightly, and the Baron flinched.

"Now, now. None o' your games. None o' your threats. You're a visitor now. A guest, perhaps. Agatha says you're even a friend. Let's put our guns down for the night."

Nox eyed the turrets on the ramparts, still focused on him. "Yeah," he grumbled. "Let's."

The Coilhunter was slow to abandon the artillery gun. To prove a point, he dropped a smoke bomb and disappeared into it, reappearing down below. He wanted them to know that he still had all the weapons he needed, right there on his belt.

"Hmm, now," the Baron said. "You look the part even better up close."

"I'm here to see your leader," Nox said. "Frank Five-eyes."

"I'm the leader here, Nox. Maybe you mean our protector, our guarantor against the ravages of the wild and the savages of civilisation. Oh, he'll wanna see you now, after what Agatha said. If they got his boy, then they got his attention."

"And what about yours? Did they get anyone you love?"

"No, I'm a bachelor of sorts. Can't ever be made tame."

"One for the wild, I guess."

The Baron chuckled. "Oh, we're all wild here, in our own way. Even you, Coilhunter. Even you."

"If you've got Frank Five-eyes' ear, then I suggest you warn him not to go to war with the other gangs. Things are already unsettled here enough. Unless you all want me to settle 'em."

"One man against an army? Oh, maybe the fabled Coilhunter could do that. But six? Naw, I think even you'd struggle with that. You might save a few, Nox, but you'd never save 'em all. Besides, the other

Farmlords'll be whisperin' in Frank's ears too, and they won't be brayin' for peace, I can assure you!"

Nox grumbled, but said nothing. He knew the Baron was right about more than one thing there. He couldn't save them all, and a lot of them would go to war. Hell, if it was Nox's kid, he would do. Why, in a way, he did. It was just a war against crime. He'd have to do some whispering of his own to bring Frank Five-eyes back from the brink. Oh, it'd have to be some whisper.

As Nox passed some of the fields, he noticed with increasing disgust that most of the workers there were children, some of them barely out of diapers. They were muddy-faced with calloused hands, toiling the soil and tending the cattle. The dark rings around some of their eyes suggested they worked long hours and slept little.

"The kids," the Baron noted. "Yes, it's not ideal, but it works."

"*They* work, you mean."

"It's a necessity in dark days."

"It ain't right," Nox said.

"No," the Baron replied, "but it ain't half as wrong as what'd happen to 'em elsewhere in the Wild North. They get food here. They get shelter. They get protection."

"And what do you get, huh?"

"Good old God-given produce."

"It ain't given by God. It's given by those kids' hands, taken by their sweat and tears."

"Well, moisture is hard to come by here, Nox, as you know."

"I can't allow this."

"Before you go messin' things up, Coilhunter, just remember what happened last time you tried to clean up these parts. You got rid of Lawless Lyle, and that just made things worse."

"Not for those who knew 'im."

"Well, what about everybody else? Life's hard here, Nox. But we're okay with that. We get by. Then you come along and life gets harder. Some o' us are left strugglin'."

"Some o' us like you, perhaps."

"Think it through, Nox. You'll be doin' these kids outta a job, outta a home. Do you know where they'd go? Oh, the Night Slavers'd have the boys, sure. You think the farms are tough? You ain't ever seen a three-year-old wedged deep in a mine. And the girls? Well, Ruby Down'd take some of 'em in, and have 'em sell their bodies, and those'd be the lucky ones. The Black Silk Collective don't treat 'em quite as well."

Nox grumbled again. That was another thing the Baron was right about. Nox'd seen some of it first-hand. He'd heard rumours of the others. Sometimes you could save them from the frying pan, but not from the fire. Nox'd learned that all too well.

"Here we are," the Baron said, after leading Nox up some stairs to the central keep. "Frank Five-eyes will see you now."

Nox smirked. "With a name like that, I'm sure he already has."

"Of course, Coilhunter. And with a name like yours, let's hope money isn't your motivation tonight."

Two guards gave the door a rhythmic knock. Nox

took a note of it, in case he'd ever need it again. He knew the rhythm he might've used would've been a little more intimidating.

"Nox," the Baron said. "Be gentle with 'im."

Nox humphed. "The fact that I ain't goin' in there all guns blazin' is gentle enough."

Chapter Seven

VENGEANCE

Nox was led through the keep to Frank Five-eyes' chambers, which were dark as death. He could only tell there was anyone in there at all by the darker shadow in the corner, huddled in a mass of bedsheets. He had short, neat black hair, gelled back, and his lack of facial hair exposed his rugged jawline, like the desert ridges without their cactus coat. His wide-set eyes were full of worry and sorrow, and behind the sorrow there was something festering that the Coilhunter knew all too well.

"Frank Five-eyes," Nox said.

There was no response for a moment. Then the whimper of a voice. "My boy."

"Your boy," Nox acknowledged. He couldn't help but think of his own. Little wild Aaron, always searching for adventure. The words knifed him anew.

"He was just a child," Frank Five-eyes whispered. "He had no knowledge of this world of ours, of this bloodshed, of these crimes."

"But you do," Nox drawled.

"No son should pay for the crimes of his father."

"No," Nox said, though he thought of how his own son paid for no crimes at all, neither his own nor his father's. He died because of others' crimes, others just like Frank Five-eyes, watching the world burn and thinking they wouldn't ever feel the flames.

"He used to watch the stars," Frank said, dragging himself towards the open window. He pointed a shaking hand to the sky. "I found out about the rocket the Iron Empire were making. He saw the design plans and was taken with the wonder of it all. He'd stare at the sky for hours, daydreamin' about travellin' to faraway places."

Just like Aaron, Nox thought. Every time, every place, he saw the parallels. Everything reminded him of that sweet little boy, and his loving sister, and his doting mother. And everything else reminded him of how quickly and savagely they were swept away. Some said it'd be the sand that got you. But for many, far too many, it was the sandstorm of crime.

"If only I could've made one," Frank said. "Some rocket to get away from this place. Maybe that's what he wanted. To get away from the sand. The heat. The God-damned guns. Maybe even to get away from me."

"Kids dream," Nox said, surprised that he was giving platitudes, when normally he just gave a round from those God-damned guns.

"I hit 'im once," Frank said. "Smack across the jaw. He bled. And he cried. God, he cried. I regretted it the moment I did it. But I never said sorry. I had my pride, you see. And my anger. The anger got me. The anger—"

"I know anger," Nox said, and he said it with fire, "but I ain't ever hit a kid."

"It'll haunt me," Frank said, and he said it as though he were telling the Reaper. For many criminals in the Wild North, when you told your dark secrets to Nox, you told it to the Reaper too.

"Good," Nox said. "Maybe it'll make you a better man."

"Maybe," Frank said. "But it won't make them better men."

"By *them*, I assume you mean the killers."

"Yes."

"Well, I got the killers," Nox said. "You could say I caught 'em red-handed."

"Agatha told me about those. You don't know they were the ones who did it."

"They admitted it."

"Folk'll admit to all sorts with you around, Coilhunter."

"Yeah," Nox said. "Even the truth."

"It doesn't matter. Even if you got the hands that held the rope, you didn't get the minds that made 'em do it. They're just the lackeys. It's the ones at the top I want."

"You'll have to gun down a lot of men to get to the man at the top."

"Well, Nox, you should know that better than most."

"I might have to stop ya. We can't have war eruptin' in the streets."

"I understand that, Coilhunter, but I can't let this go. They got my uncle, you know. Toby's namesake. And a friend of the family before that."

"And who did you get o' theirs, huh?"

"More than I can remember," Frank said. "But we let 'em have their peace, when Lawless Lyle was in charge. They're the ones who declared war. I want a life for every year my boy didn't get to live."

"And what about theirs? How many lives will they want for each year you take from them? When does it end?"

"Maybe it doesn't," Frank acknowledged. "Maybe it only ends when we end."

"Well, isn't that a waste?"

"You should know this feelin', Nox. You should know this urge."

"I do, and that's why I'm tellin' you it has to stop. Blood for blood doesn't water the grains. It doesn't fill our canisters. It doesn't make life. It doesn't save life. It just makes everything worse."

Frank said nothing. He stared at the stars. Perhaps he could see five of them up there, for each year of his boy's life. But there should've been a lot more stars in that night sky.

"What about Jimmy Tombthief?" Frank asked in time.

"What about 'im?"

"Was he in on it too? Or Wild-eyed Ernest?"

"Well, I don't know."

"He threatened my boy before, you know. Jimmy Tombthief, that is."

"I didn't know."

"He said he'd send me him in pieces in a puzzle box, like what they did to Rommond's lover. Said he'd start with the hands, so I'd know he was helpless. Said he'd send parts to my whole family." Frank paused.

"But Nox, what if he didn't just say it, huh? What if he was in on this too?"

"I really don't know, Frank."

"I do," Frank said, though it was clear he was still just speculating. "I have eyes on 'em all. The gangs. The Deadmakers. You. Hell, we caught Sam Silver in Edgetown. He was working for 'em, you know, ever since our Blood Johnson went on the run, after you gave 'im a right good spookin'. The Authentic Antiques Assembly, or All A's, as I call 'em. Grave-robbers and grave-defilers, the lot of 'em! Got a curse from it too, you know. Jimmy Tombthief lost most of his family to it. He was always jealous of the rest o' us, with our kids and our uncles and our whole extended family. He's got a daughter now, but she ain't really his."

Nox said nothing. He tried not to be jealous too.

"He's in on it, I'm sure," Frank continued. "They've got an alliance with the Good Gullet Gang and the Broken Bones Gang. Just like our own alliance with the Black Hands and the Three Wheels. Attack one and you attack 'em all."

"So don't attack 'em then," Nox suggested.

"But if they're all in on it—"

"You don't know that."

"I know it," Frank said. "I know it in my gut. In my heart. In my soul."

"And what about your mind?" Nox asked. "Do you know it there to?"

Frank said nothing now.

"You know, if you're seein' phantoms—"

"I'm not seein' phantoms!" Frank protested. "I'm

seein' the truth finally. I'm seein' with all five eyes. They're monsters, all of 'em. They have to go. They have to die! They have to ..." But Frank trailed off, still as distraught as ever. Some folk did terrible things to themselves in that state. Some did terrible things to others.

"But that's the thing," Nox said. "Vengeance ain't gonna cut it. You need justice."

"And what, Coilhunter, are you the one to give it?"

"Sometimes I'll leave it to God."

"And what if he doesn't do that?"

Nox's eyes glared in the dark. "Then sometimes God leaves it to me."

Chapter Eight

PROTECTION

Nox spent the night at the Farmlands, holed up in a ramshackle room with Agatha. They'd tended her wounds good, but she still seemed like she'd lost a few stars of her own.

"He won't listen to you, y'know," Agatha said. "You know a man's lust for the kill."

"I do, and maybe I wouldn't mind so much, but I know how that lust can lead down dark paths."

"Like the path of the Coilhunter?"

"Like the path of a massacre."

"Well, I told you they'd want war."

"And they'll get it," Nox said. "That's the problem. Both sides feel wronged. The Silent Sickles will say it's the fault of the Good Gullet Gang—"

"And the Good Gullet Gang will say the opposite," Agatha interjected.

"Exactly. And they're both right."

"And both wrong," Agatha mused.

"Precisely."

"If it were just them, it wouldn't be so bad," Agatha said. "But they have allies. The Free Farmlords are protected by the Silent Sickles Gang. With them go the majority of the iron mines, protected by the Black

Hand Gang. And then the oil wells, protected by the Three Wheels Alliance, a consortium of biker gangs that joined together to fix the prices for diesel.

"On the other side, there's the Good Gullet Gang, who protect most of the bars and saloons. With them are the Authentic Antiques Assembly, who some say have a curse on 'em from all the grave-robbin' they did. Rumour has it that they protect the Black Silk Collective, but those whore-lords won't ever confirm anything. And, of course, there's the Broken Bones Gang. A group of cripples and misfits, who mostly just protect their own."

Nox grumbled. "That's a lotta players."

"A lotta folk one wrong move away from a war. And that move's already happened. Now we just wait until the answerin' shot."

"I know you have your allegiances," Nox said, "but do you know where it'll start? I expect you'll have overheard things."

"Next you'll be callin' me Five-ears Agatha," she replied.

"Next I'll be thankin' you, and maybe so'll hundreds more Northfolk who don't die as a result."

"Well, I'm not supposed to say."

"Don't say then. Just tell me a tale. Could use a bedtime story right now."

"Well then, the story goes that the Good Gullet Gang made a deal with the Dust Barons in the Burg, givin' 'em access to all the saloons and inns there. Good money in that. Good coils. Real, whole coils. No one'd dare turn down an offer so good. This gives the Good Gullets pretty much full control of the drinkin' trade. I opposed it, o' course, not outta loyalty, but because I know it'll drive up prices for the rest o' us. You don't pay out if you don't expect to be paid more in the long run. Anyway, the Burg is teemin' with 'em now. All holed up in the same city. So, you could say the tale goes that when the sun rises, the Good Gullet Gang may be given a good run for their money."

"When the sun rises," Nox mused. "Your lot got my monowheel good, so I'm not sure I'll make it in time."

"Maybe not," Agatha said, "and I'm not sure what you'll do when you get there. But you should rest for the night. You're gonna need it."

"I'm gonna need supplies."

"We've got supplies."

Nox smiled with his eyes. "Not the ones I need."

"Your toys, huh?"

"I'll have to head back to base."

"Heard you moved it."

"Did ya now?"

"Heard you've got decoy bases all over Canyon Crescent."

"Five-ears Agatha it is, then."

"We'll patch up your monowheel for ya. As a thank you of sorts."

"It'll need more than patchin'. But if it gets me home, that's all I need. I'll have to get Oddcopper workin'. He's busy in the workshop already, but I'm not sure he's quite ready for what I need to end this war."

"Are you?"

"The Wild North doesn't wait 'til you're ready. If

you ain't born ready, you die unprepared."

"I think a lotta people in the Burg are unprepared. I think a lotta people are gonna die there tomorrow."

"Not if I can stop it."

"You can't stop an army, Nox, let alone two."

"I'll have to."

"And what about the other four?"

"I'll have to stop them too."

"It's a lot for one man."

"Maybe I'll have some friends."

"And if you don't?"

"Then maybe I'll go it alone."

Agatha paused. "Don't you ever feel lonely, this life you choose?"

"I didn't choose it."

"That doesn't answer my question. Don't you ever feel lonely?"

Nox took a while to answer. "Every God-damned day."

"Did God damn the days, Nox, or did you?"

"For the good folk, God did it. For the bad, well …"

Nox found it hard to sleep that night, not because he wasn't tired, but because he was restless. He stared out of his own bedroom window, spotting a lot more stars than Five-eyes Frank, who was blinded by his grief. They reminded him of his own losses, and the losses of all throughout the Wild North. The sky was littered with losses. The ground was too.

That's the story the night told. When day would break, it would tell the same story too.

Chapter Nine

DESERT DRIVEBY

Wild-eyed Ernest had made a home for himself in Edgetown, even though he'd promised the rival gangs he'd never settle, that he'd keep running and roaming, either to chase them or to evade the Coilhunter. He had a home now, though, and a wife and kid. Some said the Good Gullet Gang were bad, but they were good to him.

"A lovely day," Ernest said, watching the dawning sun as he flicked through his newspaper on his rocking chair. This was one of the Iron Empire's newspapers, imported illegally into the Wild North. It had the more *exciting* headlines. ROMMOND FORCED TO RETREAT. THE RESISTANCE IS CRUSHED. Some of them were lies, of course, but when books were hard to come by, this kind of thing made for some good entertainment instead.

"You're gonna be mistaken for a Regime sympathiser with that," his wife Rose said, as she came out with some lemonade in one hand and a toddler in the other.

"Ah, hell to 'em if they do think that!" Ernest replied.

"Do you have to speak like that around Daisy?"

"Hell!" the toddler cried.

"See? You'll make a show o' us with the neighbours."

"What neighbours? Everyone's still dozin' or holed up already in the saloon. And here I am," Ernest said, holding up the glass, "drinkin' *lemonade*."

"You know you can't hit the liquor after what the doctor said."

"Ah, hell to the doctor!"

"Hell!" Daisy repeated.

Rose rolled her eyes. "Should've listened to my mother. Told me to leave you."

Ernest peered over his newspaper. "Well, h—"

"Don't you say it again, Ernest!"

Ernest chuckled and turned the page.

"What's that?" Rose asked.

"Hmm?"

"All that rumblin'. I thought sandstorm season was over?"

"It is."

"Look at those dust clouds. That ain't just the dawn shimmers."

"I'll look at 'em later."

"Ernest, will ya do what I say for once in your life?"

Ernest grumbled and peered over his newspaper again. He adjusted his glasses, then stood up. "Is that one o' those bikers?"

"Oh, Ernest, you said we'd be safe here."

"We will, love. We've got a truce. Anyway, our fight isn't with the Three Wheels Alliance. It's with Frank's lot."

The biker approached from the haze.

"I've got a message from Frank Five-eyes," the biker said. "Say hello to the Devil for us." He gunned down the lot of them and sped off before the other townsfolk stirred from a shattered sleep.

"Hell," Ernest coughed, as everything went red, and then black. There was no rebuke from Rose beside him, and no repetition from little Daisy too. The lemonade mixed with the blood of all three of them.

Chapter Ten

THE DAWN OF WAR

The first blades of dawn tore through the streets of the Burg, slicing up the shadows. The shade of buildings shifted, and out came new silhouettes to line the dusty streets. They gathered in their dozens, spaced out, hats tilted against the wind, legs planted firmly, hands hovering by their hips. The Silent Sickles had taken the Gatekeepers hostage, so as not to upset the Dust Barons who employed them, but beyond that they gave everyone else in the city a gun-gaze, with plenty of ammunition behind the glare.

"Come out, you rats!" Crimson-hand Carl shouted. He drew his burnt red hand across his nose and ruffled his greying moustache. His eyes were a little manic, as if they'd seen too much, and wanted to see more. His face was puckered by age as much as he puckered the bodies of his enemies with bullets. Some called him a hired hand, but the truth of it was that he worked for Frank Five-eyes for the best part of twenty years. Around these parts, you called that loyalty.

On his left, two metres back, was Mad Madelyn, a burly woman with a wild, red mane, and a big old cleaver over her shoulder. She didn't go in for guns, and the only people who ever mocked her for it were found packaged up in pieces, if they were ever found at all. They said she started as a farmer's girl, but snapped when she lost her child to the Harvest, that fateful time when the Iron Empire came. At one time she sliced down rows of wheat. Now she'd settle for rows of people instead.

On Carl's left, two metres back as well, was All-guns Addy, decked out in fine leather, and bald as a bone. She made up for Mad Madelyn's distaste of pistols by having one in each hand, and what looked like modified multi-round pistols on each shoulder as well, fitted in a custom-made frame, with wires attached to her wrists and the triggers. She had four more on her hips, and two more strapped to either leg. Some said it was overkill, and maybe it was, but too many in the Wild North had died from not killing enough at all. Others said Addy worked a stint among the Deadmakers, that bounty hunter elite that roamed the wastes, but the Farmlords made so much money from their produce they could afford to pay her more. Another hired hand, and certainly not as loyal. But you didn't need loyalty to kill. Sometimes you paid for the guns, and sometimes you paid for the hands that use them.

Behind these were a collection of the Silent Sickles' finest, lined up in rows, spaced out to make them seem like more. Some of these were Five-eyes Frank's own kin, the ones he didn't mind losing. He would've easily traded their lives for his boy. Even now, there was a part of him hoping he still could. He wasn't there himself, of course. He was too wise for that, or too much of a coward. Well, the brave and the foolish did share a lot of graves.

The collective shadows of the gang members stretched across the widest street of the Burg, almost reaching up to the stretched shadows of the group now flooding out on the other side. They came from every tavern, bursting through the saloon doors, while some crawled out of their beds and climbed down ropes and ladders to join the growing numbers. The other people, the innocent townsfolk who rose before dawn to prepare for the busy markets, just stood frozen between them all.

"You've got some nerve, Carl!" Whiskey-eye Joe called back. He was the head of the Good Gullet Gang, and he had a glass eye to back up his name. He'd pop it out into his glass of whiskey every now and then and suck it dry. Frank had five, but Joe only need one good eye to get the job done. He had long, grease-soaked hair, with a few long whiskers on his chin to match. He was old-fashioned, so he had an old gun, but he'd gotten more than his fair share of kills with it over the years. And the thing about Joe you learned pretty quick: he had no problem blasting that thing right into your face. He'd learned first-hand of the damage it could do.

"Oh, I'm glad it's you," Crimson-hand Carl roared back. "I'll take your either eye afore I kill ya, you rotten child-killin' scum!"

"Well, ain't you a kettle, Carl!" Whiskey-eye Joe said. "We know what you did to poor Maggie. She wasn't much more than a child herself. Don't think you lot've paid enough for what you did. There'll be more. There'll be more until there's nothin' left o' ya!"

"This fued ends today," Carl said. "We'll have ya all on pikes by nightfall!"

"We'll have you hangin' by noon!" Joe growled back.

If Nox had been there, he might've said: *Let's call it even and just kill ya all.*

But he wasn't there. And the townspeople of the Burg knew it, cowering in their homes, or cowering in the streets. Something was going down there. Something bad. And the problem with bad was that it had a way of spreading in the Wild North. Folk said the sky was bad. Folk said the sand was bad. Well, those grains wafted into the city streets right then and there, adding a little mischief to the mix.

Everything went deathly silent. Even the wind held its breath. Eyes squinted. Hands hovered. Everyone was waiting for that fateful moment. In the Wild North, God always had his finger on the trigger—and boy did his finger itch.

Chapter Eleven

THE HAND AND THE EYE

It was Crimson-hand Carl who took the first shot. He blasted a hole right through the skull of the man behind Whiskey-eye Joe, just a fraction of a second after Joe shifted and dived to the side, firing as he fell.

Bullets pelted back and forth, with most also diving for cover, though a few daring sorts stayed out in the open. They didn't stay there for long. The grave was cover too, after all. Reese "Beater" Bassett, known for beating every one of his five wives, got a bullet to the knee, and soon after another to the skull. Doomteller Delilah, who liked to leave a tarot card on her victims, fell just as quick on the other side. She probably should've used a different deck.

As the numbers thinned in seconds, with heads bobbing up and down, or what looked like phantom pistols firing chaotically over the edge of barrels and barricades, Whiskey-eye Joe tried to crawl away from the fight, making for one of the houses at the side.

Crimson-hand Carl spotted him and charged after him, braving the bullets to get this higher class of kill. He bashed through the door and charged through the building, casting over tables and throwing chairs across the room, before he bounded up the stairs. The women and children inside screamed and cowered, and they screamed and cowered a whole lot more when Carl pointed his pistol at them.

"Where is he?" he roared. "Where'd he go? *Where'd he go?*"

One woman pointed a shaking finger to the balcony door, which was slightly ajar. Carl edged up to it, glancing through the crack. He saw the heel of a boot from someone dead on the ground. Maybe a husband. Maybe a father. Maybe a friend.

But not Whiskey-eye Joe.

Not yet.

"Come in here and die, you rat!" Crimson-hand Carl shouted out.

A baby in a cot across the way started bawling. None of the women had been able to make it over in time before Joe tore through.

"Shut that up!" Carl bawled in turn, pointing his gun at the crib. "Shut it up!"

One of the women hurried over and tried to soothe the child, but Carl's shouts to Joe outside just made it howl even more.

"If you don't silence that tot, I'll silence it for you!" Carl cried, turning and pointing his gun at the mother and baby.

"Now who's the child-killer," Whiskey-eye Joe said, having crept back into the room when Carl had turned. He fired, but Carl dodged, taking the bullet in his shoulder instead of his heart. He dived at Whiskey-eye Joe, taking him to the ground. He bashed his fists at Joe's face, making a bloody pulp of his features.

"This is for little Toby!" Carl shouted, as the women screamed and the baby bawled anew.

"This," Whiskey-eye Joe said, holding up a de-pinned grenade, "is for you."

The blast tore through the building, killing everyone. It sent out splinters and smoke and body parts into the city streets, where the battle waged on, and more of the Burg's townsfolk fell to the slaughter.

Chapter Twelve

THE SLAUGHTER STREETS

Only a few knew that the leaders of this particular battle were already dead, but those who did were just more enraged by it. No matter how many people they crossed off in that feud, it never satiated them. It was like asking a drunk if he'd had enough to drink.

So the streets ran red from the people who couldn't run fast enough to avoid the mob. Some died to targeted gunfire, and others to crossfire, while others yet were trampled by their own kin. A few of the more daring townsfolk tried to retaliate, reaching for their own pistols or whipping out knives. Those ones didn't last so long. Others pushed flowerpots—with desert plants, of course—from their window sills, taking out a few unlucky bandits below. Those ones fared a little better, but only because they barricaded their doors just in time.

Mad Madelyn tore through the streets, slicing at everyone in her way. She didn't care if they were innocent, if they were just random passers-by, if they were men or women, or even children. As far as she was concerned, the entire city was corrupted by the Good Gullet Gang, and by the Dust Barons too. It had to be cleansed. She was there to kill, and she was there to do it fast. In times to come, she would be called the Butcher of the Burg. If Nox let her live long enough to be called it.

Pepper Annie, one of the most well-known and well-liked of the Burg's citizens, was caught in the fray. She was old and frail, a testament to just how well-liked she was, because most others ended up on the wrong side of someone, and never got to age at all. She hobbled away from the fight and tried to push her cart down one of the side alleys.

Walnut Williams, well-known in different circles for liking easy kills, followed her into the side street. He raised his pistol, but just as he was about to fire, Cool-hand Cloe took him out from across the way. She didn't like easy kills at all, but she'd mark down Williams all the same. Pepper Annie jumped from the gunshots, unaware that she'd been so close to death. She must've been well-liked by the fates as well. Of course, in the Wild North, the fates never liked you for long.

A brawl of half a dozen gang members, all hands and fists, came down the alley at the other end. Pepper Annie tried to turn, but there was nowhere to turn to, not unless she wanted to brave the bullets in the more open street she'd come from. She yelped as one man was pushed right into her, knocking her to the ground. She huddled in the corner as her wares were trashed, keeping her hands over her ears as she screamed. Her forehead bled from when the cart was pushed back into her. All she'd ever done was get up early and sell fruit and vegetables to the townsfolk. Her husband was up north trading for more with the tribes. She only hoped that by the time he came back, she was still there to come back to.

The commotion died down with the dead, and the living passed on to the next street, either fleeing or following, but all screaming and shouting. The trader peeped her head out to look, to check that the killers had gone. But they hadn't gone. Not all of them. There was Mad Madelyn, standing as still as a statue, just waiting for another head to pop out, just waiting for another head to roll.

"No! Please, I beg you!"

"Good," Mad Madelyn said. "I like it when they beg."

Then, just as Mad Madelyn raised her cleaver for that fateful strike, there was a collective gasp from the people of the Burg. Up above, haloed by the sun, was a flying figure. Up above, and growing closer by the second, was the Coilhunter, with glider wings made into his newly-enhanced oxygen backpack, sailing in to do a little slaughtering of his own.

Chapter Thirteen

SLAUGHTERER NOX

As Nox sailed over the chaos below, he yanked a pull-string on his waist, dropping dozens of butterfly bombs on the people below. As soon as the canisters cracked open in the streets, and some on the heads of people passing by, a multitude of mechanical butterflies burst out, all seeking movement, and all carrying a noxious gas that'd knock you out in seconds. The butterflies flittered, and the people dropped like flies of their own.

It was a mercy shot, just sending those criminals and civilians to sleep, before Nox got a chance to put the rest to bed. Some said you should start with mercy, because it got harder to be merciful the longer the battle got. This was bound to be a long one.

Nox dropped right on top of one of the Good Gullet Gang, someone without a name he knew or a face he recognised, so he contented himself with a few fists to make him a little more unrecognisable. You see, Nox had a code of sorts. Only the Wanted ended up in his bucket. The rest, well, a few scrapes and bruises never hurt anyone. Sure, it'd make it easier to remember them if they posed for a poster one week later.

His drifter wings snapped shut, folding up nice and neat, as perfectly as he did it in miniature form with the butterflies or a hundred other flying toys he tinkered with on the lonely nights in his workshop. Some stopped fighting for a second in wonder, which was their mistake, as it gave the Coilhunter a little more time to mark their faces, and then, for those who did a have a Wanted poster, mark a big old bloodied hole where their faces used to be.

He cleared out that street quick and easy, slinging bullets at some and yanking others to the ground with a well-timed shot of the grapnels on his forearms. He barely had those outlaws on their knees before he strolled past and dropped another little canister from his belt. This one cracked open like an egg, and you might've thought it was something real coming out at first, if you didn't know Nox never quite took to nature. It was a snake, and it slithered out and coiled itself around the fallen criminals, expanding in length until it had their arms pinned to their torsos.

"Let me loose!" one of the gang members cried.

"Your ganglords already did that, and look where it got you." Nox paused. "Don't worry. I'll be back with bars later, unless you prefer a bucket or a box."

Nox used his grapnels to hoist himself up onto the flat roofs of the Burg, using the height to scout the next blood-soaked street. There were a lot of options, some where the gangs were in fierce fist-fighting, others where they were blade to blade, and others where it was all guns blazing. He didn't mind those streets, not for now. It was the ones with the civilians he was worried bout, the ones with the terrified traders, with the women and children. He spotted a group of shawled women dashing away from half a dozen men with that lustful look in their eyes.

He hopped down and rolled, before he was back on his feet and one of the lustful was kissing the ground instead. Then the bullets came, as they always did when the rapists never got their taste, or got a little too much of it. Nox turned and swiftly yanked a lever beneath his arm, which extended his drifter wings. The bullets pelted off metal plates made into them, protecting the women on either side of Nox. He turned sharply, and the wings snapped shut—and in the moment of the snap, he already had his pistol out and fired.

Nox took out the rest of them, heard a scream to his right, and spotted through the nearby broken window more bloodshed in the adjoining street. He dove through the window, charged through the building, and kicked open the door on the other side at just the right time to smack one of the gang members right in the face. As that man stumbled, others drew their guns, only to find they were drawing blood from their own fingers. None of these were on any Wanted posters Nox knew, so they'd have to content themselves with a lesson. You didn't want to be tutored twice.

Nox dashed up a nearby ladder and followed the sound of an explosion into the north-west district, where he knew Harvey the Hound holed up. Harvey was no friend of the Coilhunter, and a friend of convenience to the Dust Barons, but they went back, and that was saying something. Normally you didn't know Nox for long. Normally it was just the seconds of the click.

"Go on, Nox!" Harvey the Hound shouted down from his high balcony. "Beat 'em blue!"

Nox climbed up to the higher flat roofs and cleared gaps with the help of his newfound wings, casting a new, different shadow over the criminals below. Later, when folk saw a hawk or eagle sailing across the dunes, the children would wonder if maybe it wasn't an animal at all, if maybe it was Nox. They came up for a new name for him: Dunedrifter. Just another title for the Man with a Thousand Names.

Chapter Fourteen

THE BATTLE OF THE BURG

Nox took out several more known criminals when he leapt back into the main trading plaza, which was already littered with bodies. Most of the gang members fell before they even noticed him. Most were easy. But not everyone.

As Nox turned to survey the area, he spotted two he hadn't yet had the chance to greet with lead. There they were, Mad Madelyn and All-guns Addy, brawn and brains, but just as much a criminal as the next.

"Ladies," Nox said, though, of course, *ladies* was perhaps not an accurate term at all. *Killers*, sure. *Criminals*, double sure. The only thing the Coilhunter was triple sure of today was that both of them had to die.

"Always wanted me some Coilhunter," Mad Madelyn said, licking her ruby lips.

"Our quarrel isn't with you," All-guns Addy said, though she cocked her pistols all the same. When she tilted her head, he thought he saw the tattoo of a bullet on her tightly-shaved skull. Oh, Nox'd have no issue providing her with the real thing.

"Funny, that," Nox said. "You see, my quarrel is."

"Then come and get some, Coilhunter," Madelyn

teased.

"You're not the only one with gadgets," All-guns Addy said.

"I hear that from time to time," Nox replied, "but I don't hear it from the same mouth twice."

"You can't kill us all."

"I don't have to, to kill you."

Nox was ready to fire, but he saw All-guns Addy was ready first, and she had more guns cocked. He fired a token shot, but his aim was off as he dived out of the way of her four pistols. He dropped a smoke canister as he rolled, and clambered up onto the roof of a nearby building. Addy's bullets pinged dangerously close to his feet as he dashed across, and one round knocked the Coilhunter's gun right out of his hand. It was a dangerous game to run like that, but it was just as dangerous to stay still. Hell, in the Wild North, living was a dangerous game too.

Nox reached a closer roof and dived on top of them, unfurling his drifter wings to glide on down. One wing struck All-guns Addy in the forehead, knocking her out cold, but Mad Madelyn wasn't so easily bowled over. She seized him as he struck and dragged him around in a circle.

"Time to clip those wings," she said, as she snapped one clean off.

Nox reached for one holstered pistol, but Madelyn bashed it from his hand, and almost took the hand with it. He shook his bruised wrist and backed away. As brawls went, she was winning. But Nox had faced bigger foes than her before. Brawn only got you so far. It was brains that got you all the way.

But brawn was getting Mad Madelyn plenty far that day. He let loose some butterfly canisters as she bounded down towards him, but she seemed unfazed by the gas. She even chomped one of the mechanical creatures between her teeth before spitting it out. Then she smacked Nox square in the jaw, right where his mask was, and he spit more blood inside it than she leaked from the cut across her hand.

"Quite a fist you got there," Nox said.

"I got another one," Madelyn replied, before swinging at him from the side. He ducked that blow, shifted around behind her, and kicked her in the back. She stumbled forward into a nearby cart, crushing it beneath her weight.

As Madelyn struggled to her feet, Nox picked up his pistols, only to hear the scream of Pepper Annie as she hobbled towards him. Nox's arrival had helped her escape the Butcher of the Burg, but there were always other butchers to take Mad Madelyn's place.

"Get inside!" Nox shouted to the old woman, as he gunned down her two pursuers.

Then Madelyn whacked him over the head with a wooden panel from the broken cart, knocking him to one knee. Oh, she was some lady alright, but he wasn't about to make a proposal. His head spun and his vision blurred, so his next gunshot missed the mark.

Mad Madelyn seized Nox, hoisted him up over her shoulders, and hurled him through the window of a nearby building. She trundled in after him, panting heavy. He'd barely gotten to his feet before she smashed him into the wall, and then dragged him back and cast him onto a nearby table. It all happened so fast that Nox barely had time to notice his surroundings, with dozens of people packed in together, snuffing white powder, wearing eyeboxes, and shooting up to high heaven and every low hell. Where there weren't bodies, there were bags and needles.

A Hope-house.

A den for drugs.

The perfect place for a fight.

Madelyn's grip was tight around his throat. "Is that too tight?" she taunted. "You ain't much without your toys, now, are ya?"

"No," he said, the words choked. "Ain't it lucky I still have some?"

He used his elbow to crack an orb on his belt, releasing another expanding toy snake. Mad Madelyn was caught off guard when it slithered quickly up to her hands and then began to coil itself around her right arm. When it expanded to its full length, it squeezed, and boy did it squeeze hard.

She stumbled away from Nox, clawing at the clockwork creature.

"Is that too tight?" Nox asked. "It's just practise for the noose."

With that, the toy snake unfurled a little, but only to wind its way up around her throat. She tried to fight it off, but the springs worked against her. She choked and squirmed, scraping at it with one hand while reaching out around her with the other for something to help. All she did was impale herself on the nearby needles.

"Here," Nox said, taking up an eyebox and shoving it over Madelyn's face. Her gaze was instantly transfixed by the kaleidoscope of shapes and colours inside. "Take your mind off things." He wouldn't have minded that himself. Oh, how many folk'd offered. The drugs. The alcohol. The coil-shard whores. Some days it felt like it'd be so easy to give in and just forget his troubles. Trouble was, it wasn't just about him. Who'd remember the rest?

Nox strolled back out into daylight, but he'd barely squinted at the assault of the sun before he was forced to duck from the assault of gunfire. All-guns Addy had come 'round, and she'd come with more rounds in those guns than Nox could count. They had to be modified alright, a little like something he'd cook up in his workshop. See, there was some brains after all.

"Throw down and I might let you walk," Addy shouted over.

Nox'd hidden behind the broken cart he'd shoved Madelyn into earlier. He didn't fancy his chances out in the open, but he didn't fancy his chances where he was either.

"Funny, that," Nox shouted out. "Sounds like something I might say."

"Well, then maybe you know I mean it just as much as you."

Nox got ready to dash. "Folk say they mean it all the time. I'll know you mean it when you say it with gunfire."

That did it alright. She tore up that wooden cart right at the second the Coilhunter charged out from behind it. With that amount of firepower, he'd need her wasting bullets by the dozen. He leaped feet-first through a blown-out window nearby. The stone of that building would take those wasted bullets a lot better than wood. Hell, a lot better than flesh.

"Don't think I didn't see you!" Addy shouted over.

"Don't think I didn't want you to," Nox shouted back. The banter'd help. Words pulled triggers just as well as fingers. He needed her to empty at least one of those modified guns on her shoulders if he was to stand a chance. You could dodge bullets all day, but sooner or later your luck'd run out. You could guess how soon that was for most in the Wild North.

Addy puckered the outside of that building, and did a hell of a job blasting up the good porcelain inside. Again, though—better than wood, better than flesh.

"You can't hide forever," Addy called out. Perhaps she was surprised he hid at all. He was known for appearing and disappearing, sure, but he wasn't known for cowardice. And she could see his shadow stretching from the inside of the window right across to those porcelain shards.

She came closer to the opening, her hand pistols primed and ready. She unleashed another few rounds through the gap before glancing through. Oh, there was the Coilhunter's shadow alright, but he wasn't the one making it. All it was was a few sacks of grain.

"Well, howdy," Nox said from behind her.

She turned sharply, but before she could shoot, Nox fired the grapnel gun from his right forearm. The claw grabbed a hold of the wire connecting Addy's shoulder-guns to her arms. He yanked hard and fast, severing the wire, and almost pulling Addy with it.

"There," Nox said. "Back as nature intended."

"Oh, you're one to talk, Coilhunter," Addy said, her two remaining pistols raised. "You ain't anything of nature."

"Good," Nox said, pointing two of his own. "Nature's on no one's side. You see, that sun up there ain't rootin' for either o' us. It's gone and bet against us both. And the sand? Well, don't think it ain't anything but a grave. We're born in it and we live in it, and soon enough we die in it too. Here, make yourself at home in the dirt."

He kicked the dust towards her, just enough for her eyes to shift a little to look down in case he'd tapped a canister over. He hadn't. Instead, in that split moment her eyes weren't fully on him, he fired, adding a little bit of extra dust to the air. Her tattoo was just a painted target. He tattooed her brain with the real thing.

Addy toppled over, still clutching those two remaining guns. She was just half a second away from firing. You see, that's all it took. The half seconds. The quarters. The shards of time. You didn't realise you were living in fractions. You only knew it when the other guy shot first.

"Too bad," Nox said. "I kinda liked the competition." He picked up the shoulder-gun contraption Addy had used and gave it a quick inspection. He thought he might be able to employ something like it in future, though it'd need a lot of modifications.

Suddenly he heard a grunt to his left and saw Madelyn stumbling out, gasping, with the broken toy snake in her hand. She wobbled on the spot, reaching for the door frame to support her. By the looks of it, she was still seeing colours.

"You should've died in there," Nox said. "Here, let me help ya."

He unloaded a single bullet. It must've looked like something supernatural to Madelyn with where her head was right then, until, of course, it struck home right between her eyes. Maybe she could see something even more supernatural then. It took what seemed like a long moment for her to fall, but boy did she fall. The dust leaped away from her, to save themselves the guilty association.

That was All-guns Addy and Mad Madelyn ticked off the list. Pity there were still so many other names there. Well, there was one thing for sure. When they faced the Coilhunter, the last thing they'd get was pity.

Chapter Fifteen

A THOUSAND NAMES TO KILL

Nox tore through the streets of the Burg, taking out criminals just as quickly as they took out the innocent. He was just one man, but he might as well've been a thousand, because no matter where the fight was, it seemed he was there too. And then, just as quickly, he was gone again in a blast of smoke, only to reappear an alley over, or on the roofs above.

"This is Monday," Nox growled, as he smacked the butt of his revolver into the face of yet another gang member. "This is my day. This is my family's day. You made me miss it, so I'm gonna make you miss the rest of yours."

Nox cycled through the Wanted posters of his mind, looking for names, looking for faces—looking for a reason to kill. When he found them, he clicked until he clicked empty, and then he just took out another gun. Some said there were too many guns in the Wild North, but the thing of it was that there were just too many folk to shoot.

Cottonmouth Matthews. Wanted for seven murders. *Bang.*

Jasper "Jazz" Willoughby. Wanted for robbery and arson at the bank in Edgetown. *Click.*

Haybuckin' Henry. Wanted for multiple counts of rape. *Boom.*

The Coilhunter continued on, pausing just a fraction of a second long enough to let someone less familiar pass, slamming another's skull against a wall to save him the bullet. He fanned the hammer, spinning through that rolodex of names and faces in his head, finding there were always a gun-full more to file away under *Definitely Dead.*

The list went on.

Floorboards Amy. Wanted for killing her family and storing them beneath her house. *Bang.*

Thomas A. Heidenheimer. Wanted for embezzling funds from the Treasury. *Click.*

Gold-barrel Jane. Why, she wasn't wanted at all.

"Gold-barrel Jane," Nox repeated, aware that he was only repeating the echoes of his mind.

"Nox," Jane said, tipping her hat like the gentlewoman she was.

"What're you doin' here?"

"I'm here for the bounties, o' course. It's high competition in the Deadmakers. Got myself up the league tables quite a bit since you took Danny out."

"Guess you'll have to add me to the competition then."

Jane unloaded her antique gold-plated pistol, which fired more than it jammed lately. Some said that was luck, but you didn't count on luck in the Wild North. You counted on clicks.

"That's fine with me, Nox. I'm just here to pay the rent."

Nox fired two shots in quick succession at

"Mauls" Michaels, a known molester.

"There," he said, "next month's rent on me."

"Oh, I ain't here for charity," Jane said, taking out another. "I earn my way, just like the rest o' us. Well, not that you're like the rest o' us."

"No, I ain't, but I can appreciate a little bit o' law from the rest all the same."

"Pity they don't all think the same," Jane said. "A third of the Deadmakers are wrapped up in some cartel business. Another third are chargin' protection money just like the Good Gullet Gang. The rest ain't a lot less shady, 'cept they hide it better in the shade."

Jane took out another name from one of her posters. "And then there's me," she added.

"And then there's you."

"You know, you make it sound sinister when you do that."

"When I do what?"

"Repeat stuff back to folk."

"Hey, I'm just speakin' those words back. I didn't speak 'em the first time."

"Well, you make folk nervous. Still have the Deadmakers on edge after what happened with the false accusations against you and that tribal village. Not that Sour-faced Saul thinks they're false."

"He still gunnin' for me, huh?"

"He sure is," Jane said, and she raised an eyebrow. "And he—why, speak o' the Devil."

"I'd rather not," Nox said, as he spotted Sour-faced Saul rolling around the corner on his three-wheel motorcycle. "You see, the Devil's got a poster too."

Chapter Sixteen

THE DEVIL OF THE DEADMAKERS

Sour-faced Saul didn't spot the Coilhunter at first. He was too distracted by the woman at his side, a woman that looked a lot like the latest wife of Jimmy Tombthief, head of the Authentic Antiques Assembly. Of course, "the latest" pretty soon became "the late," as that crime lord tended to have bad luck with his beloveds.

And you could say that Sour-faced Saul had some bad luck of his own.

When Saul finally locked eyes on the Coilhunter, he ushered the woman away.

"Conspirin' with the enemy, huh?" Nox shouted over.

Saul humphed. "If I were conspirin' with you, sure!"

"What's with the girl?"

"None o' your beeswax, Nox."

"If you're beddin' her, you won't fare well with Jimmy Tombthief."

"If I was beddin' her, she wouldn't be with Jimmy at all. And I ain't, Nox. I'm an honest man."

"A lot of liars say they're honest men."

"And a lot of bounty hunters say you're a bounty just waitin' to happen," Saul replied. "We know your type, Nathaniel. You might say you're in it for justice, but it's *your* type o' justice. Your rules. Your laws. One day, when you crack more than you've cracked already, you won't just be the enemy o' the bad folk here. You'll be the enemy o' the good."

"That's a fine story you've told yourself there," Nox said.

"It'll be a true story one day, mark my words."

"Oh, I'll mark 'em alright."

"See, there you go again with your threats, with your intimidation. There was one name they pegged you with right. You really are a Masked Menace."

"Only to the *bad*," Nox said. "So tell me, Saul. Have you been bad today?" He eyed the woman again, aware that she was holding something he hadn't seen before. It could've been drugs. Or coils. Or something else. Something worse. Saul said he was good. So why did he consort so much with the bad then?

"One day we'll get ya," Sour-faced Saul said. "Me or one of the other Deadmakers."

"Speak for yourself," Gold-barrel Jane protested.

"I *was* speakin' for myself, Jane. And you shouldn't be standin' so close to 'im, you know. You might get hit in the crossfire."

"Well, now," Nox rasped, and he already had his gun drawn. "Is that a threat?"

"Ohoh, lookee here, he doesn't like when we do it, eh? You're a hypocrite, Nox. Down to the bone. We oughta lock you up and throw away the key. Hell, if a jail don't do, then maybe an asylum'll be a better fit for ya. Sure, I'll wear the white coat myself!"

"Oh, give it a rest, Saul," Jane said.

"I'll rest when he's dead or behind bars," Saul said, pointing aggressively at the Coilhunter.

"Say that again," Nox croaked, "but point with your pistol. Go on. Give me a reason."

"You don't need a reason, Nathaniel. You say you only hunt the Wanted, but as far as I'm concerned you just paint those posters as you go."

"Well, you're wrong, Saul."

"Well, you ain't right, that's for sure. There ain't nothin' right about ya."

"If it's just words you're slingin' today," Nox said, holstering his pistol, "I think we can part ways." He turned to walk away, but added, "I guess *Sourmouthed* would've worked just as well."

Now, the thing about Saul you knew well was that he never liked the name he'd been given. You could say he was a little sour-faced about it. So, when Nox slung those final words back, Saul's face turned ashen, and his hand reached for his hip.

Nox heard the rub of metal off leather, and turned with his own gun out just in time to blast Saul's pistol from his hand. Normally that would've done it, but Saul crouched down to pick up his gun again, and Nox was forced to shoot him in the shin. Saul fell, then scrambled up empty-handed.

"One of these days!" Sour-faced Saul shouted as he limped back to his motorcycle. "One of these days!" he repeated, as he drove off in a cloud of dust.

"One of these days, I guess," Gold-barrel Jane said with a smile.

"Yeah, one of these days he won't be limpin' away with a warnin' shot."

"He's harmless, really," Jane said, though Nox couldn't help but wonder what harm he was doing with Jimmy Tombthief's wife.

"Yeah," Nox grumbled. "Like a fly. But I don't like flies either."

"Well, you're a tinker, right? You gotta make a swatter big enough for 'im."

Nox smiled beneath his mask. "I'll add it to the list."

"So," Jane said. "This battle's over. Time for another?"

Nox holstered his pistol. "Time for a drink."

Chapter Seventeen

THE FOREVER BARFLIES

Nox strolled up to the Seven Stars Saloon, which had more bullet holes in its swinging doors than it probably had patrons inside. Now that the battle was over, the townsfolk were returning to the streets. Some were so used to violence they just kept on doing what they were doing before.

There was a gang of youths playing shoulder-wall against the tavern, passing the butt of a cigarette between them. There were some who said that was bad for you. Well, maybe that was true, but the grim reality of the Wild North was that half of those youths wouldn't make it to adulthood, and it wouldn't be the cigarettes to blame. You see, the Wild North was bad for you too.

Nox passed them by and they hid the cigarette behind their backs. He eyed them like they were the seeds of a different gang he'd have to face in the future, and he let his mask puff out its own black toxins just to prove a point. Either the cigarettes would get them or he would.

Nox pushed through the swinging doors and let the noise inside quieten to take in the thuds of his boots. Folk clattered in and out of there all day, and yet many knew the sound of the Coilhunter stepping inside. That's because he wanted them to hear. He could've just as easily made them see and hear nothing at all. And they knew that well, which was why they peeled their eyes and perked their ears all the more.

The bartender gave a nod from across the way. You could call it a nod of understanding. A drink on him in exchange for no bodies on the floor. He was already mid-pour.

"Some battle out there," the bartender said. He was known around those parts as Hands-free Hank, because the rumour was he never touched a gun. Of course, there were other rumours that said he was known by a different name in ramshackle towns farther east, where the banks were robbed at gunpoint. You did have to wonder how he got the money for the bar, but folk didn't think too much about the rum-holes. They thought about the rum.

"Yeah," Nox croaked. He downed his whiskey in one quick swig, slamming the shot glass down as if the battle were still going. "The gangs are gettin' too big for their boots."

"And you?" one of the men slouched on a stool beside him said.

Nox turned to him coolly. "And me what?"

"What're you gonna, hic, do 'bout it?"

Nox grumbled. "I'm gonna have this drink."

The man on the other side elbowed the Coilhunter. "Heard they're brewin' up for a battle at the mines next."

"You did, huh? You must have radio in those ears

o' yours."

"Funny you should say," the man replied, and he tapped a little box in his ear.

"All-ears Everett's got the goss on everyone," the other man said. "Knew my wife was beddin' the baker afore I did. Got bread for a week from it too. Didn't share a slice."

"It pays to know things," All-ears Everett said. "Ain't that right, Hank?"

Hank poured him another drink with the grumble of a grudge.

Nox leaned back and glanced from side to side, enough to capture the faces of the men lining the bar. You see, he caught your face before he caught the rest of you, and he didn't quite care if they were attached. He didn't recognise some of them, but he knew enough to know their reputation. They called them the Forever Barflies. Some said they were born with a bottle, and you can sure as hell bet they didn't mean milk. Some said they'd die with a bottle too. Well, if you didn't die to the broken shards during a bar fight, then maybe the alcohol could slowly kill you. You died by the bottle or you died by the bullet. You can guess how many tried to die by both.

That was Clamheart Carson to the Coilhunter's left, the one they said would tell you anything but a man's secrets. Some said he was a pastor in a former life, a pastor who'd had more than his sermon-share of the wine. To his left sat Dozey Daisy, the only woman of the group, who had no qualms with letting loose men's secrets as she slept at the bar. On the other side, to the right of All-Ears Everett was Whispers Stevens, who didn't need a radio to get the latest news. Everett let the radio tell him news in one ear and let Stevens tell him the rest in the other. Further on was Codex Carter, a known spy for the Resistance down south, feeding back all the intel to General Rommond.

"Where's this battle then?" Nox asked, nudging Everett.

"You know Pulleytown?"

"I know *of* it," the Coilhunter said. "They're a minin' town, right? Protected by the Broken Bones Gang."

"That they are. Said they were gonna pull it to the ground."

"Who said?"

"The Black Hand Gang, o' course."

"More miners," Nox grumbled.

"It's only, hic, half about the alliance," Clamheart Carson said. "More 'bout takin' out the competition."

"Oh, is that a secret?" Nox asked.

"Not to us," Everett said.

"And when's this attack planned?"

"Two days from now."

"Three," Codex Carter corrected. He was dealing out cards on the counter with hands of lightning. He fired a neatly stacked pile down to Dozey Daisy, who opened one eye to glance at her hand. "You in?" he asked the Coilhunter.

Before Nox could answer, Carter fired a pile of cards his way. Nox fanned them in his hand. They weren't much to play for, but he spotted the code hidden in the slightly altered symbols. *Meet me at midnight. Mason House roof.*

"He's bilkin', he is," Clamheart Carson said. "Saw 'im slippin' cards up his sleeves as if he were giftin' 'em to God."

"Damn right!" Whispers Stevens said. "He's a chiseler, that one. Oughta be wrist-wrapped in a calaboose!"

Nox cocked his head. "Well, let me know when you find a fine enough establishment for 'im where the bars ain't already bent."

Chapter Eighteen

MEETING AT MIDNIGHT

Some folk called it the witching hour. Some folk called it the spymaster's hour. Some folk even called it the Coilhunter's hour. Well, no matter who it belonged to, you'd find them all up then, pacing to and fro, mixing their brews or making their gadgets. It was just curious to see two of them up on that roof that night.

"Your intel," Nox rasped. It wasn't quite a reminder, but a demand, or maybe even a threat. You could've said it was missing part of the sentence. You could've said it went like this instead: *Your intel or your life.*

"Hell of a greeting, that," Codex Carter said. He had a scarf wrapped firm around his face, showing just his eyes. It wasn't far off how Nox did it, but Nox did it with a mask and a cowboy hat.

"Let's just say I don't have much time for pleasantries these days."

"I do, but then I suppose it pays to be pleasant in my line of work."

"And it pays to *not* be in mine."

"Touché."

"Your intel," Nox repeated. "That is your job after

79

all, isn't it?"

"Well, you know the Resistance needs it more than ever. And, by the looks of it, so do you. Well, I intercepted carrier birds rallying the forces of the Black Hand Gang, from Black Hand Quarry to the Eastern Irondelves. They're marching on Pulleytown from tomorrow at noon. Should reach them two days later. That gives you the better part of three days to make it there first. Hope you've got that big old wheel of yours."

"I do, but it's pretty busted, and my spare needs a new engine first."

"A bad time to walk."

"A bad time to do anything," Nox corrected.

"What'll you do then?"

"I don't quite know yet. Still got the first battle ringin' in my ears."

"Save them, I guess," Codex Carter proposed. "I wonder, though, why you don't just leave them to it. Let them cull each other."

"I would, if that was all it was. But it ain't just about them. It's about everyone else caught in the crossfire. Look at what they did to the people of the Burg. It's the same everywhere. Innocent folk get caught up in it all the time."

"It'll be some task, though, trying to save so many."

"Don't I know it. You see, I know how much it takes to keep a man alive, and I know how little it takes to make 'em dead."

"You do know that pretty well, that's for sure," Codex Carter said. "We could use you, you know."

Nox smirked behind his mask. "Did Taberah send you to recruit me?"

"Not as such."

"Not as such, huh?"

"The Scorpion can be quite persuasive, you know."

"I know."

"She told me once she'd persuade people in life, or she'd persuade them in death."

"Well, let's hope we won't be chasin' ghosts again," Nox said.

"I guess that's a no then."

"The war down south is yours to fight. I've got my own up here."

"It's getting serious though."

"I heard.

"We're pushin' as far east as the early days. This could be the turn of the tide."

"Well, let's hope it turns for ya. It won't do much for here. The Wild North was always wild. And it'll stay wild if you go knockin' on the Iron Emperor's door."

"You're not gonna tame it then?"

"I'm gonna try," Nox said. "But maybe I can only tame a few."

"You'll have to tame more than a few to stop this war of theirs."

"Ain't that the trouble. See, maybe I should be recruitin' you."

Codex Carter smiled with his eyes. Usually, it was the Coilhunter who did that. "Not enough good men in this world, huh?"

"Ain't that the truth."

"Well, I don't think you'll find much more up there with the Broken Bones Gang. Though they aren't half as bad as the others, or so the intel goes."

Nox humphed. "Well, a half-rotten apple still ain't somethin' you wanna bite."

"Touché again."

"So," Nox mused. "Pulleytown."

"It's out of the way," Codex Carter said.

"In the Wild North, what isn't?"

"More than normal, I mean. You'll have to go through the High Valleys." He handed Nox a wrist map, with a route marked out. It had little dials on either end to scroll the map up or down as you went. "That's climbs and drops by the dozen. Do you have the gear for it?"

Nox cocked his head. "If I don't, I'll make it."

"Well, don't get overconfident, Coilhunter. You know what they say about nature here."

"Yeah," Nox said. "It's just another criminal too."

Chapter Nineteen

THE HIGH VALLEYS

Nox wasted little time setting out. He packed his things, paid for some extra supplies, and hired a horse to get him to the monumental network of cliffs and valleys in the north-eastern section of the Wild North. They called them the High Valleys, because the ravines dipped down deep where old rivers ran, carving out valleys in the cliffs. But they were still cliffs, dropping even deeper on the other side.

The journey was easy at first, with the land so flat and empty, but Nox knew it'd get tough soon enough. He also knew the horse wouldn't be able to go all the way. He'd have a choice then: park it somewhere and hope he could make it back in time before it froze at night or died of hunger, or send it back the way he came, and maybe he wouldn't quite make it back himself. How we wanted his monowheel then. You see, it couldn't kick the bucket if it was half bucket itself.

They say *slow and steady wins the race*, but those who said it must've been foreign to the Wild North. If you were slow, the gunslinger fired first. If you were slow, the scorpion stung swift. If you were slow, the rattlesnake gave you a kiss of venom before you could run. And, well, if you were slow with the coyotes, they'd drag those slow limbs of yours back to their ravenous young. You could be steady, but you couldn't be slow. Not against those marching gangs. Not against Death himself. No, *quick and ready* was more the Coilhunter's style.

So Nox tired that horse out as much as any desert drifter, even more like one searching for a watering hole. Nox had plenty of that, of course, having paid the Dust Barons' taxes, on top of the Dew Distributors' seemingly ever-increasing prices. He tired the horse out even more with that big vat of water on his back. But, you see, it was either that or carry the coffin instead.

The night wore on, and it wore them with it. Nox gave the poor old mare a break and his own limbs a stretch as he strolled alongside her. He'd grown more fond of horses since Old Reliable, not that he didn't like them before. He just didn't like them getting shot and killed because he was riding them, because he was a target and the outlaws needed more target practice. Some would've said that's why he didn't have a family either. But he did have a family. He never stopped having a family. You see, the bodies can die, but the link doesn't. The feelings don't.

"I miss 'em," Nox said. Maybe he was saying it to himself, or maybe he was saying it to the horse. He knew sure as hell he wouldn't be saying it to anyone else. He couldn't afford to be vulnerable with the vultures. He couldn't afford to be weak with the wayless. He had to be everything the criminals feared, everything they dreaded, everything that kept them up at night. He had to be everything but a man. He didn't have the luxury to feel, to shed tears, to break bread and be merry. He couldn't be a man of flesh. He couldn't be a man with feelings. He had to be machine. A monster. A mirage. He was the Coilhunter. Nox. The man died with Nathaniel Osley Xander. He died with his family.

The horse didn't judge. The horse didn't hate him like the conmen did. The horse didn't run from him like the criminals did. The horse just trotted on, oblivious to the laws and lawlessness, oblivious to the troubles of men. Oh, how some up there tried to live that life too. The quiet life. The carefree life. Some fled the war down south, or fled their past, or fled their fears, or fled even their own happiness. Some of them were found in the Lostlands. Most were never found at all. It was different for horses and men. That horse was bred for travel, but Nox was bred for something else. The Wild North was his breeder, and it bred him for battle, bred him for bullets.

"Well, let's get back on the trail," Nox said, climbing back on again. There was no bounty box at the back, just that big old jug of water. Besides, there wouldn't be a big enough box for who he'd have to kill.

Nox saw the silhouettes of the High Valleys not long after the first colours of the morning formed in the sky. Some said those colours would tell you the fortune of your day. Well, was it any wonder then that Nox so often saw red? The cliffs were monstrous, towering over the landscape, protecting some from the sun's evil glare. Nox primed his pistol as he drew close, all too aware of how the dark places tended to house dark things. Nature was pretty when she wanted to be, out in the glisten of day, or by the candle of moon. But she could also be ugly. The ugly things tended to hide in the cracks and crevices, just like the outlaws of the Wild North.

Nox eyed the shadows warily as he passed. Whether it was man or monster in there, he had pebbles in his guns for either of them. Or maybe it was just shadows. Well, he'd gun those down too, if he had to. You could've called him paranoid, but he'd seen and experienced too much in the Wild North to ever not expect the unexpected. Folk said the land was alive. Well, then, what would they say about the shadows too?

He spotted the first earthen steps that led to a rocky ramp along the side of one of the cliffs. He glanced around for other landmarks. Two lonely cacti stood like scarecrows nearby. He inspected the map Codex Carter gave him, and noted the two cactus symbols.

"I guess this is it then," Nox said. He hoped he was right, because he couldn't afford another long journey down and a search for other cliff-ramps along the monumental desert wall. You might've said he was lucky he stumbled into Codex Carter (though he more often strategically "stumbled" into you), but Nox made his own luck. He made it with cogs and springs and wire. And he either added it to the display shelf back in his workshop, or he added it to his arsenal.

"Up now," Nox urged. The horse was a little

flighty here, and the Coilhunter couldn't blame her. That ramp wasn't much to stand on, and wasn't wide enough for a misplaced hoof. But it was cool, at least. The sun was already painting the rocks with the shades of day, but it hadn't quite reached in there yet. It'd be setting in the west before it started painting Nox with sweat. By then, he hoped he'd be off the cliff-face and into the valley dips on the other side.

He got about halfway up, zig-zagging back and forth along the eroded walkway, when there was a break in the passage. The horse might've made it, but Nox didn't feel like taking that chance, and clearly the mare didn't either.

"Well, old girl, I guess this is where we part ways." He patted her fondly, gave her some food and water, and sent her back down the cliff edge. It was a long way down, and there were two ways to do it. He watched for a moment like a parent, like he watched little wild Aaron on his first pony ride. Oh, he'd had bullet wounds and knife wounds, but they never cut so deep. With that horse gone, there was no one there to say "I miss 'em" to.

He continued up, hopping across the two-foot gap. He followed the cliff walks, which were wide in places, but narrow in most. Every now and then the scree tumbled down from above, like the marbles of the gods, intent on making him slip. And sometimes the cliff itself gave way, and Nox had to scramble to get his footing, and not become just another bit of scree to line the path of a wanderer below.

Nox passed some graves made into the rockface and paused to read their names. They weren't the telling monikers of the Wild North's criminals. They were simple. *Tom. Alice. Manuel.* Simple names for simple folk. Who know what they'd call them in the afterlife?

He'd missed Monday. He'd missed his family day, that time he drove back to the little graveyard on the road to Copperfort, just outside the jurisdiction of the Wild North. That day was sacred, a reminder of what he'd lost, and what he was fighting for—to ensure no one else felt that loss again. Yet no matter where he went, he found other reminders, just like those cliff-side graves, that no matter what he did, he just couldn't save them all.

"I can at least try," he found himself saying out loud. As much as he judged the criminals and the conmen, some might've said he judged himself more. He tried to save the people of the Wild North, because he'd failed to save his own family. You see, you didn't need ghosts then. He haunted himself with that every single day.

Nox continued on, climbing the swiftly sloping staircase of the cliff, hugging the rock. You didn't hug the rock for comfort. You hugged it to avoid the discomfort of nature hugging back. The tribesfolk might've communed with the land, and some even said they tamed it, but Nox had no tribe, no ritual for the earth, no ceremony for the sand. He made every step across the Wild North with the grim assumption that the land didn't like it. More often than not, it seemed like he was right.

He spotted what looked like a waterfall far ahead, plummeting down into a deep basin below. He thought it was a mirage at first, until he saw the iconic architecture of the Dew Distributors around the lake below, all curves and waves in stark contrast to their box-shaped armour.

As he approached the waterfall, which fell in steps, he saw a rocky bridge that crossed right over it. Normally he'd expect to see Dew Distributor guards there, what with how easy it might've been to just dangle a cup over the edge and take a sup without making a sum. But this was the High Valleys. Nature stood guard instead.

Nox filled his canister as he passed, though he threw a quarter coil into the waterfall for good luck. You see, you didn't accept gifts from the Wild North. You paid for them now or you'd pay for them later. There were those little graves on the cliff-side to prove the point.

Nox paused for a brief rest on the rocky bridge, supping from his newly-filled canister. He watched the tiny figures far below, bottling water and keeping guard. They ran a tight ship down there, because there was always more demand than supply. Some folk said one day the water'd dry up, and you'd have to sell your house for a bottle. But for now, at that waterfall, it seemed like it'd keep on flowing.

Nox reached back into the water behind him to top off his canister, when suddenly something seized his arm and pulled him in.

Chapter Twenty

THE DEW MONSTER

It happened so fast that Nox barely saw what it was that'd tugged him under. He thrashed in the water, fighting the gorge as much as the monster that gripped his arm. Everything was a blur of blue and white and grey. He choked and gargled, gasping for momentary breath as his head briefly pierced the surface.

He felt the rush of the water pushing him closer to the edge, and yet the tug of something else pulling him back. Whatever it was, its grip was tight. He felt the circulation cutting off in his right arm. He bashed at it with his other fist, but it didn't loosen.

Then he saw the creature more fully, and he knew it saw him back, because it had one large eye in the centre of its domed head, a hide like grey leather, and many more tentacles than he could count. One of those wrapped around an outcropping in the middle of the water, keeping it steady against the push of the fall.

When Nox saw that giant eye staring at him, and was only glad he didn't also see a giant mouth, he grasped a canister from his belt and pelted it right into the iris. He wasn't sure what he'd grabbed, but by luck it was a flash orb. The white blast momentarily blinded it, and Nox slipped free from the creature's grasp.

And then the rapids seized him.

As Nox dropped over the edge, he fired one of his grapnels up. The claw scraped at the rock beneath the flood, but came back empty. Nox fired the other, and this one tugged tight. He dangled for a moment, but before he really got his bearings, he felt the wire pull tighter. A tentacle had wrapped around the grapnel and was pulling it and the Coilhunter up.

"Hell," Nox said, as he was dragged back over the edge of the waterfall. "What is this thing?"

Oh, it answered. It answered with a sharp, swift pull on the wire, which yanked the Coilhunter back into the water. He flailed in the froth, trying to see a target, trying to reach for his gun. The grapnel swung back suddenly, but just as quickly a flurry of tentacles leaped at him and pulled him towards the creature's anchor on the outcropping rock.

It pinned his limbs quick. One of the tentacles wrapped around his neck, choking him. Another wrapped around the tubes leading to his oxygen tank, dislodging them and exposing his scarred lungs to the dust of the desert air. He coughed and choked, and the black smoke from his mask turned grey.

This was it, he thought. This was how he went out. Not one-on-one with a gunman. Not in a chase across the desert wastes. No, he'd die to something he didn't even have a name for. He'd die to something that didn't even know he had a thousand names.

No.

Just at the brink of giving up, just like the brink of that rocky precipice, a different kind of flood struck the Coilhunter. They say your life flashes before your eyes in the moments before death. That was often when many saw their greatest regrets. For Nox, he saw his family perish, and other families perish, and his own quest for justice. More than anything, he saw it wasn't over. It wasn't done.

He summoned whatever strength he had left and yanked his arm down towards his hip, just enough to graze the pistol. The tentacle pulled back, so Nox had to fight it harder. The strap holding the gun in place was just millimetres out of reach. He scraped his fingernails against the strap, never hating leather quite so much. The edge of one fingernail caught a frayed fiber. Yeah, this'd be a battle played out in millimetres and threads. And maybe you didn't quite see it, but perhaps a battle played out on that scale in life as well. The strap tugged, but it stayed firm. The button was like the lock of a Treasury safe. It didn't budge. It didn't give. It didn't loosen. He needed just a little more, just a tiny store of strength. More than anything, he didn't want his grave to read: *And the leather won.*

Maybe it was a newfound strength, or his sinews tearing, or his shoulder coming loose from the socket, or maybe it was the creature shifting against the shove of the deluge, but he got the tip of one finger under the strap and pulled. It opened, and he seized the gun, though he didn't have much strength left now to hold it.

He tried to curl his arm up so he could bring

the gun closer to the creature's face. Oh, it took everything he had. The sinews and muscles were close to bursting. As he fought, that creature just stared at him with that one big, monstrous eye. It knew it had him. It knew he couldn't win.

But Nox stared it down too. He only hoped he could soon use the barrel of the gun.

The tug-of-war seemed to go on forever, his arm pulling up, the creature's limb pulling down. He could've fired now, but knew he'd only get one real chance at this. He had to make it count. He had to make it kill.

His vision started to fade, and for a moment he thought that was it, that he'd lost all control of his muscles, and he was back where he started, with arm down at his hip again. But his vision cleared just as quick, and he saw his flexed arm still pointing that gun up. He just needed a moment more, another inch, another twist, another click.

Bang.

The bullet tore through the creature's eye and into its brain, if it had a brain. The tentacle grip loosened almost immediately, and Nox gasped for breath, before realising that the monster's clutch of the rock had loosened too. Nox grasped at the outcropping just in time before the water could flush him away.

The tentacled creature slumped over the edge and plummeted down into the basin far below. No doubt the Dew Distributors saw it. Perhaps they reacted with horror. Or perhaps they knew that beast, or others like it. If the rare waters were filled with monsters like it, then perhaps some folk were wise to fear one day the waters would run out. And perhaps others were wiser to fear what happened if they didn't.

Nox didn't rest there, and didn't dare refill his canister. The water didn't need guards, because it already had some. He limped away, reconnecting his tubes. He felt the rush of the chemical mixture into his lungs. Not just oxygen, but the pain-numbing vapours too. Oh, those helped more than ever now.

As Nox continued on his journey, a little more torn and battered than before, he cursed nature, knowing all too well that nature cursed him back.

Chapter Twenty-one

PULLEYTOWN

And there it was, at last, after many slips down the scree-laden valley paths, and the winding walks, and the periodic flats.

Pulleytown.

It was a grey beacon on the horizon, spewing out smoke from its many tall chimneys. As he drew closer, he could see why it go its name. The entire settlement, carved into the valley, was cobwebbed with wires. Buckets and coal skips zipped along those lines, and here and there a person dangled precariously from a ziplined chair.

And it was as much a sight to behold up front than it was at a distance. The old mines were now homes, sectioned off from one another, some with round windows and doors, others square, and others yet more randomly shaped. Each of the doors was painted a different bright colour, which was about the only hue at all there, for everything else was dark and soot-covered. The criss-crossing network of travel wires, without any sense of order, blotted out some of the sun's rays in sections, while in other places the sun shone down like a spotlight, often illuminating deep drops into other sections of the caverns.

Nox strolled through the town, glancing up at people ziplining overhead. One sat in a bucket, with only one leg dangling over the edge, while another seemed to have no limbs at all, and was strapped in from his torso. Some worked, and some played, and others seemed to be almost part of the machinery itself. Everywhere there was the clang of metal. They woke to it. They worked to it. They ate to it. And they slept through it, as others toiled the mines at night instead.

"Mr. Wacky!" one of the kids exclaimed, running up to Nox. She pointed at him and kept pointing, as if he was a freak of nature. In some ways, he was. In the Wild North, a lawman was always a freak of nature.

"That ain't my name," Nox said as he strolled on. The other townsfolk paused to watch with wary eyes.

"It isn't?"

"No."

The girl scratched her head. She'd been certain before.

"Where's Mr. Quacky?" she asked.

"He's busy."

"Busy?"

"He's workin'."

"Oh." She paused. "Workin' at what?"

Nox grumbled. "Where can I see your leader?"

The girl scratched her head again. A man, presumably a relative, ran up to her and dragged her away. He pointed nervously at the door painted red. Yeah, that was about right. Red was always the colour that Nox knew best.

He rapped his knuckles off the wood. The door

opened almost immediately, with a teenage boy in a wheelbarrow on the other side. His legs dangled over the edge. There were a lot of folk with dangling legs there, if they even had any legs at all.

"Yes?" the teen asked.

"I need to speak to your leader."

"Who will I say you are?"

Nox cocked his head at the question, which was lucky for the youth, as more often he'd cock his gun. "Tell her to guess."

The teen worked hard with his hands to roll that wheelbarrow away. He had help with a series of ramps inside the tunnel, letting gravity do most of the work. He'd left the door open, so Nox just walked on through.

"He never gave a name," Nox heard the teen shouting inside.

"Then go back and get one, Wheelbarrow Bob!" came a woman's voice.

Nox followed the voice and entered a large cavern chamber, with many people around.

"Nathaniel Osley Xander," the woman in the centre said.

"You can call me Nox," the Coilhunter replied as he drew up close enough to inspect her.

There she was, the leader of the Broken Bones Gang, the matron of that makeshift family: Iron-chair Ivy, strapped into a mechanical chair, with two chimneys at the back spouting steam, and small landship treads below for moveability. Her black locks were longer than her limbs, and they coiled around the chimney stacks and armrests, with still more to fall down both shoulders.

On either side were dozens more in chairs, or hanging out of zipline seats, or suspended by their shoulders, or held up by metal frames. Some were missing limbs, while others couldn't see or hear, and others still couldn't talk, and those were grouped others to help them. All of them had a disability of some sort, but not a single one of them was coddled. They all had the soot of the mines on their hands and faces. Everyone worked the same.

"All of 'em are my family," Iron-chair Ivy said, as she noted Nox's stares. "We're the broken, the abandoned. Do you know what the Regime would do to us, what they've already done? So we came up here."

"To rob and kill."

"To live. And sorry, Nox, but you can't live here without robbin' and killin'."

"The people you robbed and killed can't, sure."

"We're not bad folk, Coilhunter. We've just been dealt a hard hand. We're playin' it like the rest o' ya. Etchin' out a livin' from the rocks."

"Well, maybe you should've stuck with etchin', and not made an alliance with the Good Gullet Gang. The Black Hand Gang are after your mines—"

"They always were. We left them one a decade ago, when we came up here. Wasn't worth the fight."

"Well, now the fight is here, Ivy. I presume the Good Gullet Gang has asked for your support?"

"They have, and we agreed to it, what with us never goin' back on our word, but we haven't made a move yet."

"Looks like you won't have to. I have intel that the Black Hand Gang will make a move first."

Ivy perched up in her chair. "I thought they'd wait. I thought they'd let the Three Wheels Alliance do more hits first."

"Well, they ain't waitin', and neither can you. I see you've got a lotta children here."

"Some of 'em were abandoned by their parents," Iron-chair Ivy said. "Blame that war down south for that, and all those rumours about folk only givin' birth to demons now. Some of 'em were your so-called 'normal', and some of 'em couldn't walk or hear or see or speak. Their parents took that as proof they were demon spawn. They left 'em in dumpsters, Nox. They discarded 'em like trash. Just like so many do to us. That's why we took 'em in."

"You have to get 'em outta here," Nox said.

"We know, Nox."

"Then why ain't you doin' it?"

"Because this is their home."

"But they'll die here."

"We know that too."

Nox shook his head, but couldn't find the words to say.

"You don't understand, Nox," Ivy continued. "They have nowhere to go. Their birth parents won't take 'em back. Their so-called families won't. No one else wants 'em. No one else will fight for 'em. If we send 'em off somewhere, what do you think'll happen? If the Black Hand Gang doesn't get 'em, then the Three Wheels Alliance will. So many folk think they can come up here to the Wild North and just keep runnin'. But we can't, Nox. We've got nowhere to run to."

"Well, if you won't run," Nox said, "you better fight."

Ivy seemed more grim than ever. "We intend to."

"I'll be here," Nox said.

"Another ally."

"No. I ain't no ally, because no matter what good you do for some, you do bad for others. Just because I don't have a poster for you yet doesn't mean I didn't hear enough about your kills. I'm not here for you. I'm here to stop the innocent from dyin'. That means by your hands too."

As Nox turned to leave, he spotted a young man near the door, with both hands missing.

"What happened to *your* hands?" Nox asked.

"Dust Barons," the youth replied, with the nervousness of one who thought the Coilhunter might've taken them otherwise.

"Let me guess," Nox said. "You stole somethin'."

The youth looked away.

"Now, why ain't I surprised?"

"He stole an apple," Iron-chair Ivy said. "Don't you tell me that's justice."

The Coilhunter paused. "No, I suppose it ain't."

"So, tell me what is, Coilhunter?"

Nox glowered at her. That well-timed puff of black smoke burst from his mask. "Me."

Chapter Twenty-two

A FORBIDDEN LOVE

As the Coilhunter made his way back through the tunnel, a woman of about eighteen or nineteen rushed out to him from an adjoining chamber.

"Coilhunter," the young woman said.

"Yes?"

"You do jobs for money, right? For coils?"

"Don't we all?"

"My beloved is Henry Askilles. They call him Double Dice Henry, 'cause of his gamblin'."

"I've heard of 'im. One of the Black Hand Gang, if I'm not mistaken."

"You're not. We've been forbidden to meet or marry. We've been forbidden to love!"

"Sounds wise, with that feud o' yours."

"But it's wrong! We're in love, Coilhunter. Doesn't that mean somethin'?"

"Maybe it does," Nox said, "but for all these gangs, it seems hate means more."

"Can you get 'im outta there? I can pay you. I can pay you a lot."

"Folk don't pay me to save people. They pay me to kill 'em."

"Oh, but please, Coilhunter! Can't you do me

this mercy? Can't you do this for love?"

"There ain't no Cupid here, girl. There ain't no bow of love, ain't no arrows to make it all alright. You want love, you gotta load up your sixshooter instead. So load up, girl, and get firin'. There's maybe even a bullet meant for your heart. I know there's one meant for mine. Maybe one day they'll find a way to fire it. Well, until then, I'm still waitin'."

Nox heard the trundle of iron wheels and saw Iron-chair Ivy rolling down the corridor. She didn't have to use her hands to move her chair, as it was all automated. The steam puffed from the exhausts at the back.

"She tryin' to rope you into her wicked web?" Ivy asked.

"I don't know," Nox said, turning to the besotted woman. "Is it wicked?"

"How can love be wicked?"

"Stop bein' a fool, Harmony," Ivy said. "He's after yer iron, not yer heart!"

"I knew you wouldn't understand, ma. I should've never told you."

"This sounds like family business," Nox said as he turned to leave.

"Wait," Ivy said, grabbing his arm. "Whatever she offers you to save Double Dice Henry, I'll pay you double that to kill 'im."

Chapter Twenty-three

MEN IN THE MINES

Night wrapped the sky and smothered the stars. Pulleytown was quiet. The machinery of the mines were turned off. No one sang in the saloon. No one played music. No children laughed, being accustomed to staying up late with their adopted parents there. No, Pulleytown had the appearance and sound of a dead town. A ghost town. Nox hoped that wasn't an omen.

In the far distance, there was the glimmer of lights. You might've thought at first that they were stars, if you didn't realise just how much smoke Pulleytown pumped into the heavens above, obscuring everything. And besides. Folk said the stars were the souls of your kin. Night smothered those stars for a reason.

"It's them," Iron-chair Ivy said, peering through a spyglass. "I can sense it."

"So can I," Nox said.

"With their pitchforks and torches, no doubt," Ivy continued, "for us so-called demons and monsters, and not-quite-men."

"It's not too late to get the children out."

"It is, Nox. It'd be suicide to do it now, in the thick

of night."

"It might be suicide to stay."

"Well, then, at least we'll die together, in our home."

"Don't think that a noble death," Nox rasped. "So many others have died the same way."

"Well, they'll lose dozens of their men before they get inside the mines."

"And then?"

"Then they'll lose dozens more."

"But they have dozens of dozens. How many do you?"

"We're just over a hundred total here. We lose some and gain some."

Nox grumbled. He knew they wouldn't be gaining any that night.

The rumble of trucks above rocked the caverns below, where the children cowered. They were holed up in deep delvings, but the men who were coming were miners too. They knew how to delve, and they knew how to reach them.

A few periodic explosions could be heard outside. Those were the land mines dotted around Pulleytown. It was a little bit of cold irony that the men who came to kill the so-called cripples might end up with a missing leg or arm of their own. Some folk loved their irony, and some just loved their iron. The fates paid you with the former, and folk paid you with the latter, or paid you with lead.

The sounds came closer, showing that the Black Hand Gang had pierced the outer perimeter. The land mines couldn't be used too close to the tunnels or they might cave them in. Those men outside knew that too. There were hundreds of them, flooding the town, perching outside doors and windows, guns at the ready.

Nox waited in the main tunnel, watching for the shadows cast on the walls by the torches. Those shadows would tell him everything. They'd tell him who was coming. They'd tell him how many. They'd tell him when to reach for his hip or his belt. Nox remembered facing monsters in the mines back when he was chasing Handcart Sally. This time it was men. The question was: which was worse?

The first half a dozen charged around the corner. They didn't see it, but Nox had one of his grapnels hooked to the far wall. He pulled it taut as they ran through, tripping the first three. The others tumbled into them, forming a nice, neat pile of outlaws. Nox made a few neat piles too sometimes, but they weren't usually alive when he did.

"Good o' ya to pay a visit," the Coilhunter drawled. "But you're supposed to knock first."

He wrapped his knuckles off a nearby switch on the wall, and a weighted net fell from the ceiling, pinning the piled men in place. Nox crouched down beside them, and they froze in their struggle.

"Now, don't let me find you further in the mines," he said. "Consider this a warnin'. I ain't gonna warn ya twice."

He was about to stand up and leave, when he spotted one familiar face in the pile-up. It was Bowler Bronson, the greatest coil counterfeiter in the Wild North, or so he claimed, and the former chief of

Black Hand Quarry. He'd been deposed after the Coilhunter's prior confrontation with him, and was now just a lowly goon. He looked pretty low now on the ground, pinned beneath his fellows. But in the Wild North you could always go six feet lower.

"Well, howdy," Nox said.

"This is just … a … a misunderstandin'," Bowler Bronson lied.

"No, I think I understand ya just fine. See, you got away last time, and hell, I didn't quite mind. Thought you'd turn over a new leaf, but here ya are with five o' your finest, wearin' that old leaf thin."

"They're not mine. I swear!"

"Oh, some honesty at last. Did ya learn that from Honest Pete? I know James "Ironking" Dalton runs the Black Hand Gang now. Surprised he didn't kill ya. Are you surprised I didn't kill ya too?"

"But I did nothin' wrong!" Bronson protested.

"And there you go lyin' again. See, I saw your face on a poster in the Sea o' Sorrows. Yeah, they don't just go up in the Bounty Booth now. You killed Swill Roberts when you couldn't pay your tab, and almost took out his barmaid to boot. He was under the protection of the Good Gullet Gang, you know. And more than that, he was under the protection of the law."

"He had it comin', Nox. Tauntin' me for losin' Black Hand Quarry. He had it comin'."

"And guess what," Nox rasped. "*You* had this comin' too."

He flung his pistol and fired, sending Bowler Bronson's blood all over his compatriots. They screamed and tried to recoil, but the net held them tight.

"See, I warned 'im once already," Nox said, before standing tall again. "As I said before. I ain't gonna warn ya twice."

Chapter Twenty-four

THE MONSTERS IN MEN

The next group of gang members came through, but they saw their netted fellows, and then saw the shadow of the Coilhunter further on. Some turned and ran, while Nox fired his grapnel at one and yanked him into the tunnel, before knocking him out with the butt of his gun.

"The Coilhunter's here!" one of the fleeing men shouted. There was a flurry as men struggled against each other to flee the tunnels. Their shadows made a mockery of them on the tunnel walls.

Nox waited for the next wave, but they didn't come just yet. Nox was primed and ready, and growing impatient. He knew they were wise to fear him, but the outlaws were very seldom wise. Many would march on with false bravado, right into his wire, or his net, or that smoking barrel.

But not these. Not yet.

Come on, little flies, he thought. *The web's waitin'.*

He heard a gruff voice, the sound of a few well-placed slaps, and then a commotion as something heavy and metallic was put in place. Nox saw the shadow of it on the wall, but couldn't quite make out what it was.

"What about our guys?" one voice asked.

"Leave 'em."

Nox edged out past the netted criminals to investigate, keeping close to the wall. No doubt they saw his shadow stretching out to greet them, but they didn't tremble, and that other shadow never budged.

Then he saw it.

A mole.

A tunnel digging machine.

Hell, Nox thought. Oh, that mole could get him there alright. It could dig right down to the fires beneath.

The machine powered up. Its rotating, dome-shaped and diamond-tipped drill spun into action, blasting out a ferocious din. It was pointed right at him, as if that tunnel hadn't yet been carved. Oh, it wasn't there to make a tunnel. It was there to bore right into him.

He ran.

That machine monster came after him, pushed by the other gang members behind, who steered it down the path of the tunnel. They could've made themselves new ones. But no. Taking out the Coilhunter was worth more than any gold or iron.

Nox hopped over the netted criminals as he fled, then skidded to a halt as he heard their cries for help. The drill wasn't going to stop for them, no matter who their families were, or their friends. It was going to make minced meat of them, before it did the same to Nox. He was planning on letting them go with a warning, but their own kin weren't planning on that.

The Coilhunter charged back and desperately

pulled at the net to get them free. The weights kept them pinned, but it wasn't just that. They had little prongs that burrowed into the earth like moles of their own, and latched deep below. They were made to hold you down. You weren't ever getting up.

Nox grabbed a knife from his boot and sawed at the rope. Every frayed thread seemed to take a lifetime. The drill turned the final corner to face them all.

"Please!" the men begged. "Help us, Coilhunter! Help us!"

"I'm tryin'! I'm tryin'!"

Nox sawed one of the strands, but the opening wasn't big enough yet. One of the men reached his arm through and tried to brute force his way through the rope.

"You're makin' it harder!" Nox said, as he half fought with the man as well as the yarn. He sawed another section of the rope clean through, but still it wasn't enough.

The drill was close now. The buzz of its rotating blade shook the caverns and shook their bodies. Oh, but those men were already shaking.

"Help us!" they screamed. "*Help!*"

Nox sliced through another strand. The drill was just inches away and pushing closer.

The knife was blunting. The rope seemed tougher now. The drill was on them.

One man's foot was caught in the tunneller's blade and ground down to nothing. His scream was terrifying, and it only spurred the others to fight one another to get out of the tight opening Nox had made, and was still desperately trying to make wider.

One of the men popped his head and arm through, but couldn't fit the rest of him. Nox kept on sawing, kept on fighting with the threads. And the drill kept coming.

He knew they weren't going to make. Increasingly, he worried he wasn't going to make it either. The domed blade came dangerously close to his face as he sliced desperately at the rope.

And then the flurry of fighting limbs knocked the knife from Nox's hand, right under the approaching drill. Nox couldn't reach for it without losing his hand, and then his arm, and then the rest of him.

All he could do now was back away.

"Help us!" they screamed anew, as the spinning blade came down on them.

Nox reached for his hip, but the man who was half out of the net grabbed at his legs and pulled him to the ground. Nox was forced to kick at the flailing limbs to free himself, to not get pinned in the path of the advancing machine.

He freed himself just in time and stumbled backwards, and scrambled on the ground until he found the safety of an alcove in the tunnel wall.

Nox watched with horror, then looked away as the tunnelling machine tore right through those netted figures, turning the tunnel red. He didn't even have time to pull his gun and end their misery. The tunneller ended it for them, but made it too.

It passed on, down the tunnel, unaware that Nox was hiding in the alcove. He could've sprung on the others now, but he wanted to know who the man with the gruff voice was. By his reckoning, it was James "Ironking" Dalton. The man who had no mercy for his kin.

Now, the question was asked before. Which was worse? Monsters or men? Well, some folk said they're all monsters. Especially the men.

Chapter Twenty-five

A WAR OF WIRE AND LEAD

Nox waited for the tunneller to fully pass before he crept out of the tunnel, over the mess of body parts, and out into the streets of Pulleytown, if they could even be called streets. He stalked the shadows, pulling a few lonely guards into the darkness.

"I want 'im dead!" a voice boomed. A gruff voice. The voice of the Ironking.

Nox could see him clearly now. A man with more mutton chops than face, as black as the iron he craved. His head was bald, except around the edges, and he had a big old nasty scar across the back, from when he was struck by a falling support beam in the mines. Well, these were new mines to him. Nox was keen for him to have another accident.

"Save Ivy for me!" the Ironking roared. "I wanna carve 'er up myself."

Nox darted through the shadows to get a better view, and a better aim. He knew James Dalton from the posters. He'd worked his way up to the top, and not without working up a tally. By all accounts, he was worse than Bowler Bronson. He worked closer with the Night Slavers to get younger boys for the mines. And he worked closer with the Iron Empire too, churning out their iron currency.

Nox came close enough to prime his shot. If Dalton had had a crown, he might've blasted that off first. But no, just a head. Oh well, that'd do.

Just as Nox clicked the trigger, someone spotted him, and another gang member leaped at Dalton, dragging him to the ground. Nox tried to get another shot, but dozens of the Black Hand Gang charged at him.

He tried to cast a butterfly canister their way, but they swatted the capsule to the side and it didn't break open. They dived at him, and he couldn't see their faces clear enough to gun them down. He fought, fist and foot, but they pulled him to the ground and piled on top of him. Yeah, they didn't even need a net.

He scrambled on the spot, reaching out for the unopened capsule just inches away. Everything was just out of reach. Just like life, when you were tussling with Death. His fingers prodded it away a little further, and he thought he'd never reach it. And then another hapless gang member who raced over kicked it right into his hand.

Nox smashed the capsule on the head of one of his attackers, and the mechanical butterflies streamed out. They latched onto the faces of the scrambling figures, blasting out their noxious green gas. They conked out, some slumping away, while others dropped right on top of him.

Nox managed to turn enough beneath the weight to face the sky, where the moonlight and starlight edged the wires overhead. He pointed his one free arm up and fired the grapnel. It locked tight around one of the wires, and yanked him up, sending the stacked figures into the air in all directions.

As Nox dangled on the wire, he glanced around for James "Ironking" Dalton, but he was nowhere to be seen. For now, at least. Nox did what he always did when the outlaws fled. He made a note of where they ran, and another note to follow them. *Next time I see ya, I'm gonna gun ya down.* As he swung along the wire back into the mines, he added another thought: *And that ain't just a bounty. That's a promise.*

Inside the mines, the Black Hand Gang were tearing up the place. They bashed through doors and broke up the furniture. If they'd found any of the Broken Bones Gang, they might've broken more of them as well.

But they didn't. The tunnels and chambers seemed empty. Even the main room, where Iron-chair Ivy was known to hold her meetings, was vacated.

"It seems they fled," one of the Black Hand Gang said.

"Damn," another replied. "Dalton wanted to make a mess outta Ivy."

"Tell him to try!" Ivy shouted, as she rolled swiftly down a ramp from a tunnel high in the wall. She fired at them with her shotgun, and wheeled over another who didn't fall swift enough to her gun.

The Black Hang Gang charged into the chamber, but just as quickly came the groan of wires as dozens of the Broken Bones Gang swung down in buckets and skips, or ziplined across in harnesses, guns blazing.

The attackers turned to the ceiling, firing at the

figures that zipped across the wires. Most of the Broken Bones Gang swung away from the bullets, but every now and then a body slumped still overhead.

On the ground, Iron-chair Ivy and a group of other chair-bound or wheelbarrow-bound outlaws swept through the chambers, firing just in time to save one of their wired companions, or clenching their eyes as they fired just in time to save them. But not everyone was saved by another. A few bodies dropped dead in their chairs as well.

A large iron skip swung sideways into a newly-emerging group of attackers, bowling them over and knocking some out cold. Inside, a group of youths pelted the survivors with rocks and coal, often with just one arm to lob them. They didn't fire the iron. You saved that for the living, not the dead.

Most of the remaining Black Hand Gang fled back down the tunnels. Iron-chair Ivy rolled after them, blasting them with her shotgun.

"Get outta here, you scum! Out!" she roared.

Nox ziplined across the town, through a high tunnel, and found himself in the main chamber once more, watching as Iron-chair Ivy and her posse squared up against the Black Hand Gang below. By the looks of it, they could put up a fight, and put down a life.

Nox landed on one of the ledges above, just in time to grab one of the enemy gang members by the shoulders and throw him over the edge. It would've been a big drop, and a quick death, were it not for the passing coal skip on the wires below. The man plucked his blackened face from the coal and bashed his fists, sending soot into the air.

Another criminal grabbed Nox in a bear hug, pinning his arms. He struggled for a moment and almost toppled over the side with his attacker. Then suddenly Wheelbarrow Bob trundled down a nearby ramp, knocking the other man over, and almost sending Nox over too. It wasn't quite a rescue, as the Broken Bones Gang wouldn't have minded seeing the Coilhunter out of the picture too. But for now, he was an ally. You thanked God for that, even if it was only temporary.

Nox heard a boy cry as he was snatched by one of the criminals. He didn't kick, because he had no legs to do it. That made him an easier catch, an easier kill. The Black Hand Gang didn't mind getting their hands a little dirty. They could soot them black or paint them red.

Nox yanked the grapnel from his right forearm and hooked it on the wire overhead. He pulled down to test it, then leaped over the edge. The hook cruised down the wire, Nox dangling beneath. As soon as his feet touched the ground, he unhooked, turned sharply, and smacked the criminal in the face with the hook. He toppled to the ground, still clutching the kid with one hand, but now clutching his face with the other. Oh, he'd have scars alright, but then so did Nox.

"Didn't your mother teach you right and wrong?" the Coilhunter croaked. "Didn't she teach you not to snatch the innocent? Well, you got a smack on the cheek for that one. Don't make me teach you with lead."

The criminal pushed the boy away, scrambled up,

and ran. They all ran. In the Wild North, even when you settled, you were still running. Running from the Regime. Running from the Resistance. Running from your conscience. Running from the law. Some called Nox the Dustrunner, but they were all dustrunners up there, running from Death as well.

Chapter Twenty-six

THE POWDER KEGS

The Black Hand Gang didn't just have thugs and thieves amongst its members. It had miners, who dug and built the iron mines throughout the region. They knew those tunnels. They knew what held them up. And they knew what'd tear them down.

Three figures entered the tunnels, dynamite in hand.

They called them the Powder Kegs, and boy were they explosive.

There was Short-fuse John, who knew explosives like the back of his hand, and would give you the back of his hand if he as much as thought you were looking at him wrong. Then there was Close-call Larry, who lost three fingers because he liked to hang around for the bang. And finally there was Soasa Sanders, the Dynamite Lady of the Resistance. Except she was dead, or so the reports from the so-called "Civilised South" said. This Soasa Sanders was an imposter, dressed in her clothes, with her short hair and belt of dynamite sticks. The Powder Kegs wasn't just a name though. It wasn't even just a job. To them, blowing up stuff was life.

So, they rigged those mines to blow.

Short-fuse John rolled out wire, while Soasa piled dynamite around the wooden support beams holding up the roof. Close-call Larry hauled in TNT crates and gunpowder kegs on an iron pull cart.

"You should probably be one of 'em," Short-fuse John said, "what with that handicap o' yours."

Close-call Larry held up his right hand and wiggled the remaining thumb and index finger. "Hey, I can still grip things. Hell, I'm sure I can still pull more pins than you. I lost my fingers. What's your excuse?"

Short-fuse John was already getting riled up. "My excuse? I formed this group, you good-for-nothin'. Ran explosives for the Resistance before there was even a Resistance, back before the demons came. We had the real Soasa then. She'd have had your mouth filled with dynamite to save us your yammerin'. I might have to do the same."

"I'd give you the finger if I still had it," Close-call Larry said. "Wait. Here, I've got another one."

"Stop bickerin', you two," Soasa said. "We have work to do."

"Who are you to give orders?" Short-fuse John asked. "You ain't even the real Dynamite Lady. You'd still be workin' in the Ruby District if it weren't for us."

"Yeah, and maybe I shoulda stayed there," Soasa said. "Are we here to talk or blow things up?"

The reminder helped unite them in the mission. After all, it was all about the bang.

Chapter Twenty-seven

THE BANG

The first explosions rocked the mines, collapsing the entrance and sending new plumes of dust into every still-standing chamber. Some of the oil lamps blew out, adding darkness to the murky haze.

"Oh God," Iron-chair Ivy cried. "They're blowin' up the mines!"

"We've gotta get out," Nox said.

"How?"

"I was hopin' you'd have an answer for that. What about the wires?"

"They won't hold us all."

"They don't have to. They just have to hold a few."

"And what about you?"

"I'll find a way."

"You've been good to us today, Coilhunter," Ivy confessed.

"Well, don't go readin' my eulogy just yet. And don't think I won't be bad to ya if I find your face on a poster."

Nox helped Ivy's gang onto the wires, starting with the young. They crammed those coal skips until the wires groaned anew. Others used the buckets and harnesses, and Nox had to take down some of the dead already in them first. He might've said they could bury them later, but when those tunnels blew, that'd be burial enough.

The next round of explosions pushed further into the caverns. The smoke and dust flooded the main chamber, making everyone except the Coilhunter cough and cover their eyes. He already had his goggles on for that, and his mask filtered out the dust.

"Go!" Nox shouted. "There's no time now."

The skips and buckets and harnesses zipped away, but there were still a few others on the ground, including Iron-chair Ivy, Wheelbarrow Bob, and two children who hadn't made it to the wire lifts in time.

Nox grabbed a hold of the two kids and fired a grapnel up to the wires.

"I'll be back for you two," he said.

"I ain't leavin' this chair," Iron-chair Ivy protested, as she fanned the smoke away from her face. "We'll find another way."

Nox zipped across the wire, dropping the children on the other side, where some of their kin were there to lead them out. He turned back, and was ready to jump down to where Ivy and Bob were last seen, when another blast rocked the chamber. It tore through the far wall that held up the wires, sending them down into the avalanche of rocks and dust below.

Then I guess ya ain't leavin', Nox thought, and he wondered who'd now lead the Broken Bones Gang.

"Coilhunter!" one of the kids shouted. They pulled at his arms, urging him to follow them. He raced through the adjoining tunnels, smacking his head off overhead beams. He lost his hat to one, and knocked down oil lamps with his shoulders. The tunnels were becoming narrower. Those kids could fit through just fine. He might've played with toys, but he was no kid.

"Quick!" the children screamed.

Oh, Nox'd been quick. He had the bruises to prove it. But swiftness wasn't going to get him out of there. He reached a section where he was forced to crawl. His steel-plated guitar bashed and twanged off the ceiling above.

Another explosion rocked the chambers behind, sending reverberations down the tunnels. The scree fell on him, like the first dirt cast into the grave. Oh, they were more than six feet under now. And that tunnel was growing tighter by the second.

He shimmied forward on his elbows and knees, until finally the passage was too small for him. He saw the leg of one child vanishing through the narrow tunnel. They were used to that, to squashing through the gaps, to the suffocation and claustrophobia of it all. It didn't matter if they were afraid. They were small. That's all that mattered in the mines.

"I can't get through!" Nox shouted. It was an odd sensation to feel a little helpless now, to scream to the children ahead as if they could somehow save him. You see, you could spend your days saving others, but there was a guarantee of sorts in the Wild North: one day someone'd have to save you.

"Take your gear off!" they shouted back.

Nox took off his guitar, paused for a moment to think if he'd leave it behind it or send it ahead of him, and then shoved it through the passage, where a child's hand grasped the neck and pulled it through. Oh, if only Nox were as slim as that guitar, even if he had to be pulled through by the throat.

"The oxygen tanks!" the kids roared.

Nox paused a little longer on that one. "I need 'em to breathe!" he croaked back. Oh, and maybe he'd croak if he had those tanks disconnected for too long, but he'd also croak in the cave-in if he didn't get through.

He struggled in the passage to get those tanks off his back, and had to take his mask off too. Few had ever seen him without the mask. Few had ever seen the scars beneath. But pride was a dangerous thing. You see, pride was an ally of Death.

He took one last gasp from the mask, then pushed the oxygen tanks through the passage. The kids grabbed them and pulled them through.

"Come on!" they yelled. "Hurry!"

Nox scurried through as far as he could, but then he jammed. Even without most of his gear, it was still too tight, or he was too fat.

"Argh!" He fought the rock around him, twisting as best he could to see if that'd help. It didn't. That just seemed to wedge him tighter. He felt a different tightness in his chest as the dust got into his nose and mouth, and then into his lungs.

He heard the sound of pickaxes on the other side, and glanced through to see the children working ferociously at the rock, making a bigger opening. But they were small. The older children and adults had disappeared down some other passage, no doubt one for bigger folk like him.

But it was too late to go back.

Another blast rocked the tunnels, sending smoke and dust right down to where Nox was. He coughed and choked on it. Oh, how he craved his mask now.

He shifted back down the tunnel a little, just enough to move his arms. He unhooked both grapnels from his forearms and hacked at the rock with them, using them like pickaxes of his own. He struck that rock like the old folk searched for gold, and the new folk searched for iron. But he was searching for breath, for life.

Another boom came, and this one seemed louder. The dust was thicker and darker now, clogging his goggles, and clogging his lungs. He coughed in fits and spurts, and had to tear off his goggles to see a little better. The debris stung his eyes as he continued to mine his way through.

And then there was a rumble that seemed far too close, and he knew this time he couldn't stay there. He let the grapnels hook back into their launchers and shoved himself through the opening, using every ounce of speed and strength he had. It was still tight, and the kids still hacked away on the other side, but his shoulders dislodged some of the blockages, and he tumbled into the larger chamber on the other side.

Just in time.

The next blast collapsed that tunnel, sending a fresh spray of dust through. Nox coughed and spit, and wiped his face with a handkerchief. The kids didn't back away when they saw the marks on his skin. To them, he wasn't a monster. To him, they weren't either.

"Now what?" Nox asked, as he reconnected his oxygen tanks.

"The tunnels!" the kids cried.

"More tunnels?"

They beckoned him on to another set of passages, this time lined with tracks. Some of the children were already departing in coal carts, heading deeper into the iron mines.

"Oh, not these again," Nox said.

You see, the first set of tunnels were just a warm-up. These ones were the real thing.

Chapter Twenty-eight

THE TRAIN OR THE TRACKS

Nox clambered into the nearest cart, kicking out some of the coal. His guitar was already in there, held close by one of the children, who only had one arm to hold it. He didn't play it. He knew it was sacred to the Coilhunter. These kids were kind. Unlike the other gangs, they were taught respect.

But respect didn't matter if you were dead. Nox still feared that they and he wouldn't make it out in time.

The kids worked the levers on that cart like magic. No. Like a job. They knew that place inside and out, and more than anything they knew the labour. Some of them even had a few muscles to prove the point.

"Let me," Nox said, and they didn't protest. His own arms were tired, but he was sick of the mines, and happy to do anything to get out of them. He glanced back at another boom to see the previous chamber disappear in dust.

"Duck!" one boy cried.

Now, in the Wild North, when someone screams *duck*, it can mean one of two things: one, that the Coilhunter's fabled pet was perched nearby, ready to roast some eyeballs; or two, you better get your head down quick, or something was about to strike. Well, it was the latter now.

Nox ducked seconds before he would've been knocked out cold by the jutting support beam.

"Let us," the kids said, taking over the levers again. They could work them and keep their heads lower than the Coilhunter. Nox had to almost lie flat to not have his head ripped off by the rock above.

"How do you do it?" Nox asked. Of course, it was a silly question, because they never had a choice. They didn't choose to be "broken." They didn't choose to be abandoned. The only choice anyone ever made was when Iron-chair Ivy let them in.

The cart plummeted down a steep decline, gaining speed. The track screeched beneath the wheels, and rocked from the rumbles of the blasts behind. Some of the track was on solid ground, but a lot of it was held up by beams from the adjoining walls. If any part of it was reliant on supports in the stone behind them, they'd all go tumbling down into the depths below.

Nox heard the heaves and pants of someone to their right, and spotted a familiar figure sliding down a ramp into the tunnel next to theirs. He could see Wheelbarrow Bob through what seemed like windows in the wall, some formed naturally over the years, and others delved by the miners to help offload the carts.

"Get in!" Nox shouted.

He watched as Wheelbarrow Bob struggled against the flat of the adjacent tunnel, only seeing him from the periodic gaps. His hands were blistered from his frantic fight with the wheels.

"Hurry!" Nox roared, but no amount of words would make those wheels spin faster. He was mostly keeping up for now, but he had to get ahead, or the tunnels would have to cross, if he was to have any chance of joining them. The cart stopped for no one, and the booms behind them didn't either.

An explosion blasted through part of the other tunnel, shaking the ground and sending down dust from the ceiling. Nox could see that it was about to give.

And just as it did, and just as Wheelbarrow Bob appeared at another opening, Nox fired his grapnel at the youth. The claw tore a hole in his shirt, but it was better than his skin.

"Hang on!" Nox shouted, before he yanked the grapnel back. Bob grabbed a hold just as he was pulled, wheelbarrow and all, through the gap. The barrow plummeted into the depths below, and Bob almost went with it. He dangled at the side, screaming, as the cart continued on.

Nox let the grapnel recoil, and pulled to help the youth ascend faster. And then the tunnel narrowed, with two great walls on either side, right in Bob's way. He climbed up the wire, but his hands were raw from earlier. Nox pulled him up from above.

The walls came, and Nox dragged the teen over just in time.

The youth panted as he splayed in the cart.

"What'll we call ya now?" Nox asked, as he heard the clatter of the wheelbarrow deep below.

They continued on, down through more tunnels,

as the previous ones collapsed behind them. After a while, they emerged into the dark of night again, with a lot more stars in the sky. They were in a deeper valley now, where the tracks led to carriages that served some of the other towns in the area.

Even from here, they could see the smoke rising from the plateau of Pulleytown. The tunnels were gone. The caverns were gone. So many people were gone too, buried deep beneath the rubble. Pulleytown lay in ruins. As far as the Black Hand Gang were concerned, if they couldn't have it, then no one could. Not that it'd stop them digging through later. Greed wasn't temporary. It lingered, like the ghosts of the dead.

As Nox surveyed the damage, he thought of the one who ordered it: James Dalton. The Ironking.

"I have to go back," Nox rasped.

"No! You'll be killed."

"Maybe I will, but I've gotta kill someone first."

You see, you could be the train or the tracks. You couldn't be both. Folk said some were born to be run over, and others were born to do the running. The conmen and criminals were often the trains, knocking down anyone in their path. Well, you could be the train, but that didn't mean there wasn't another one on an intersecting course. A train of justice. A train called Nox.

Chapter Twenty-nine

THE IRONKING

The Black Hand Gang dragged Iron-chair Ivy out from the mines. She'd survived the collapse and was found down one of the side tunnels, half-buried under the rubble.

"Now, who's this?" James "Ironking" Dalton asked, as he patted an iron bar in his hand.

Iron-chair Ivy tried to crawl away, dragging her feet behind her.

"Oh, you crawl, girl," Dalton teased. He turned to his fellows. "Look at her go, boys. Now, I like a girl on her knees, but not like this."

He followed her and stomped on her legs, pinning her in place.

"Come on, now," he continued. "You didn't work up those arm muscles for nothin', now, did ya?"

She tried to scramble away, tugging against his weight.

"You think you're a big man, don't ya?" Iron-chair Ivy said. "Standin' on the women, on the broken, on the poor."

"She speaks!" Dalton yelled, turning to his companions. "Thought for a moment, girl, that that mouth o' yours didn't work either. Maybe we should put it to the test."

"You can rape me and kill me," Ivy said through her gritted teeth.

"Oh, we will."

"But you can't break me."

"You're already broken, girl. Ain't much use for ya now." He turned to another gang member and nodded. "Pin 'er up."

Four men seized her by the limbs and carried her to Dalton's truck. They pinned her to the bonnet, holding her down. The headlights flooded the ruins of the town, highlighting Dalton as he approached.

"You coulda just given us Pulleytown," he said. "We asked ya nicely before. But this war the Good Gullet Gang and Silent Sickles Gang started, well, that's a good reason to ask ya rough."

He banged the metal bar down on the bonnet, making her flinch. Then he grabbed her thighs and rubbed his hands down them.

"You don't feel that, do ya?" he taunted. "I do wonder if you'll feel it later."

He grabbed her ankles and yanked hard to the sides, forcing her legs open.

"Ya ain't even pretty," he said. "And you won't be anything at all when I'm finished with ya."

"Neither will you," Nox said, as he appeared from the shadows behind them.

He fired his grapnel at the surprised Dalton, smacking him right in the face. Dalton stumbled, grasping at his busted nose. The hook recoiled, just in time for Nox to kick the man who attacked from the left, and fire a shot to the knee at the man on the right.

The gang members blasted the area, but the Coilhunter vanished into the smoke left by his steel-plated guitar. He reappeared elsewhere, smashing heads off the side mirrors of vehicles, and sometimes straight through the windows. He couldn't gun them down, but that didn't mean he couldn't give them a headache.

He disappeared again, and the gang members shot up their own vehicles, sometimes even their own kin. Dalton still fumbled on the spot, clutching his face with one hand while pointing with his other at every shadow he thought was the Coilhunter.

The smoke faded from one location, revealing what looked like a snake on the ground.

"What's that?" one asked.

"A rattlesnake!" another replied.

But it wasn't quite a snake, and it didn't quite rattle. It expanded in length as it slithered towards them, staring at them with those little beady eyes. Those painted-on eyes.

"It's one of his toys!" a third man yelled, and he said it with the fear they all felt now.

The gunfire was more hectic this time. They fired at that toy snake with everything they had, but it slithered out of the blast of most of them. When they finally clicked empty, the toy snake was coiled up dead. Well, in as much as toys can die.

In the flurry of it all, no one saw Iron-chair Ivy roll off the bonnet and crawl across the ground towards Dalton. She grabbed his legs and tugged, pulling him to the ground. He turned and kicked at her, then scrambled to his feet.

"I'm the Ironking!" he roared, with the blood still rolling down his face.

"Then here," Nox said, appearing behind him again. "Have some iron."

He clattered Dalton with the iron bar he'd used before, sending the blood spraying from his ear. Dalton needed both hands now to hold both wounds. When the Coilhunter was through with him, he'd need many more.

Dalton collapsed to the ground and tried to get away.

"It's your turn to crawl," Nox said.

And boy did he crawl. He shimmied away on his elbows as if he'd never used his legs before. Well, he'd never use them again.

Nox seized him and threw him onto the bonnet of his truck, that same place the Ironking was going to defile Ivy. Nox fired a warning shot at the other gang members, who were out of bullets and out of breath. They backed away.

"Now, you could've fought fair," Nox said, as he unstrapped a grapnel launcher from his arm and used the wire to tie Dalton's left wrist to the side mirror. "You could've fought with honour," he continued, as he used the second grapnel to fasten Dalton's wrist on the other side. Nox let loose another warning shot at the gang members parked in a circle farther back.

"You know how this goes, Coilhunter," Dalton said. "This is the Wild North. There ain't no fair and there ain't no honour."

"Not for you there ain't," Nox replied, as he held

up the iron bar. It glinted in the moonlight. "But a boy can learn."

He smashed it down on Dalton's right leg. The audible crack was heard by all, and Dalton screamed. Nox didn't need to fire a third shot to make those gang members back away a little further.

"Now," Nox said, as he cast the iron bar into his other hand. You see, he had two gun hands, and he had two for this iron bar as well. "Did ya learn somethin'?"

"Go to Hell, Coilhunter!" Dalton spat.

"You first," Nox said, as he smashed the iron bar over Dalton's other leg. The crack and the cry were even louder this time, and the crowd retreated further. Some of them were already running, while they still had good legs left to run.

Chapter Thirty

DOUBLE OR NOTHING

It didn't take long for the Black Hand Gang to vacate Pulleytown. Nox could've pursued them, could've chased them down, but he was tired. He let them take the Ironking, as a warning to the other gangs. You see, sometimes dead just didn't cut it. Some feared being broken more.

Nox helped Iron-chair Ivy into one of the abandoned vehicles.

"Don't expect me to drive it," she said.

"I don't. I expect you to wait. I'll drop you off where the kids went, before I go get some rest."

"You deserve it, Coilhunter."

"Pity the criminals won't be so obligin', huh?" He turned and looked at a few he'd tied up. Some just had to hang around. "Let me deal with these ones."

He slammed the door and patrolled the area, seeing if he recognised any of them. You see, it was easier if he did. He had plenty of bullets still left in his guns, and plenty more in his belt. You didn't really cull the gangs if you didn't do a little bit of actual culling.

"*Slasher Sandra*," Nox said, as he finally found one. "You carved up a few families in Oldtown real well. Well enough for some to see ya. Well enough for some to get a real good picture of your face."

"Loosen my bonds and I'll do some work on yours," she barked in response. "I'll make ya smile real wide!"

It just took a little flick of the wrist and he gunned her down. The other captives flinched as she toppled over.

"Who's next?" Nox asked.

He strolled through the others, pausing every now and then to glance one over. He did a double-take at one.

"Don't I know you?" he asked.

"I don't think so."

"Why, that's Double Dice Henry," the other captured criminal beside him revealed. "Give 'im a game and he'll play for coils. Give 'im one of the Broken Bones Gang and he'll play with 'em too. Oh, he'll play real nice."

Henry eyed the man with fire.

"And I guess you're Loose-lipped Somethin'," Nox said.

"Scissors Thompson is who I is."

"Like I said," Nox rasped. "Loose-lipped Somethin'."

Nox taped up Thompson's mouth to save him spilling anything else. Oh, that was some mercy, because you could spill the beans or you could spill your guts. Either way, in the gang world, it all ended the same. By the rope or by the bullet.

Nox crouched down beside Henry. He eyed the man up and down to see what Ivy's daughter saw in him. He'd barely come of age, by the looks of it. He'd tried to grow a beard, but hadn't quite managed well. He still had the pudgy cheeks of youth

"I'm supposed to save ya," Nox said.

Henry smiled at that comment.

"And kill ya," Nox continued.

Henry frowned at that one.

Nox stood back up and circled Henry's position. "You've got one gunnin' for your heart." He paused. "And one just gunnin' for ya. I guess it all comes down to the flip of a coin. Or the roll of a die."

"Oh, I know how you roll 'em," Henry said. "Painted the same result on all sides. Sure as hell loaded 'em too."

"Well, I loaded these," Nox said, holding his two revolvers to the criminal's face. "Now, give me a reason to let you live."

"Now, there's a gamble!" Henry said with a laugh.

"You should go all in on this one, Henry, because it might be the last gamble you make."

"You gonna break my legs too, huh?"

"To start with, sure."

Now, there were times you put on a brave face, and times you let them see you cower. Nox had seen a lot of brave faces on the posters, but when he found them, when he was through with them, they all cowered the same. He crouched back down and let his mask puff black smoke into Henry's face.

"Well, what'll it be, Henry? You feelin' lucky?"

Henry was young, so he didn't have the wisdom of age to temper his bravado. But you didn't need to be old to fear the Coilhunter. The children feared the boogeyman. The criminals just feared Nox.

"Well, now, let me see," Henry said. He mulled things over by chewing his mouth. "Could give ya intel, maybe."

"I've got intel."

"Do you now? Suppose you know about me and Harmony?"

"Henry and Harmony," Nox mused. "Has a ring to it."

"Oh, don't give her any ideas. She'd have a ring already if it weren't for Ivy."

"You're not givin' me a reason. You're wastin' my time. You're wastin' your life."

"I'm about ready to make a point, Coilhunter, if you'd give me a moment to make it."

"Well, here's your moment."

"Well, see, Harmony's my love. What's that lass o' yours?"

Emma, Nox thought, but instead he said, "I ain't got a lass."

"Sure ya do. Oh, you know the one. Ha-handcart Sally, right?"

Nox eyed him coolly.

"She's yours, right?"

"She's her own."

"So I hear."

"Well, what about her?"

"She used to rob the iron mines, right? Well, don't think her name won't be on the list for the Black Hand Gang. Old Blood Johnson might've had her bought and paid for, and that came with his protection, but he's long gone, and protection don't mean anything right now."

"The Black Hand Gang are done," Nox said.

"Oh, we're culled, sure. But don't forget that we've got allies."

"The Silent Sickles are done too."

"And what about the Three Wheels Alliance? You taken out every biker in the Wild North, hmm?"

"Not yet," Nox rasped.

"Well, you better get there quick if you wanna save her. I say they're only days away."

"What makes you think I wanna save her?" Nox bluffed.

Double Dice Henry smirked. "Those two kids o' yours she's got with her."

Chapter Thirty-one

HANDCART RANCH

A ranch stood at the base of a mountain range in the north, straddling tribal territory. It was said that it belonged to the tribes once, and it was bartered for. The price, no one quite knew. Folk gambled on the rumours of how much she paid for it, but they didn't gamble on the name. They called it Handcart Ranch, because it belonged to Sally Hays, better known as Handcart Sally.

She had three horses outside, and had others she trained and sold. She didn't barter for those. She paid for them with coils. The biggest was hers, an Ootana horse that spooked easy. The other two, smaller in size, and brown and grey, were for the smaller members of her household: Laura and Luke Mayfield.

Luke sat in the armchair in the corner of the room, beneath the west-facing window. He liked that one, because it gave him more light to draw by in his notebook in the evenings. Some said he had a gift for art, and Nox was one of them. Art was rare in Altadas, due to the Iron Empire's culture ban. Some of it could be found in Resistance hideouts or in abandoned culture caches, and the rest was smuggled into the Wild North, just like Luke.

"Stop yer drawin', Luke," Laura said. "It's dinner time."

"I'll be there in a minute."

"You said that five minutes ago."

"Well, I'll be there in six then."

"It's gettin' cold, Luke. Mama wouldn't like you eatin' cold food."

"Don't call her mama. She ain't our mama."

"She is too. More than … more than …" Laura didn't finish what she was going to say. It'd been close to a year since it happened, since they found their mother in the Rust Valley, creating monstrous amalgamations of human and machine. Since Laura had to kill her.

"I'm doin' my drawin's," Luke protested. He dug the charcoal in fiercer, creating a darker black. He'd been drawing a lot in black since it happened. It was as if he just couldn't see colour anymore. Laura said it'd pass. But it hadn't. Time had passed, but that was it. Some said time'd heal you. But you have to remember, time is trying to kill you too.

"You're the man o' the house now, Luke," Laura said. "You gotta act like it."

And he was, sure enough. A proper ten years old now. A man, by his reckoning. By his father's reckoning too. Of course, his father's reckoning was a gun barrel to the core. A gun shot by Gun-shy Luke. The memory was black, just like the charcoal. And in the notebook of the mind, sometimes you just couldn't ever turn the page.

"Leave me alone," Luke said. He'd been alone a lot since it happened, even though Laura and Sally were around. He spent time with his horse, Chestnut, but otherwise he sat and drew the mountains, or the spartan patches of trees, or something from his imagination. He didn't like that the land was so plain, because it left more for his mind to fill in. He didn't like what he drew to fill the blanks.

"Help me with the gravy, Luke," Sally called from the other room. He'd helped her before with that, half because he helped himself to seconds when dinner was served. She knew he was finicky about getting it the right texture. Not too thick and not too thin. She tried to get him into cooking, like she did with Laura. Laura took to it no bother, reminding him of his mother. He didn't like the reminder.

"He won't budge!" Laura yelled back. "He'll become part of the chair, I tell ya."

"Don't you say that!" Luke shouted. "Sally, she's sayin' it again." He didn't like that remark. He didn't like any suggestion of merging with something inanimate, just like his father had, just like his mother had made his papa into a monster.

"Cut it out, you two!" Sally shouted back. "Here, Laura, help me set the plates."

"I set 'em last time," Laura said.

"Well, you can set 'em again."

"But *he* doesn't do anything."

"Leave 'im be, Laura. Just help me set the plates."

Laura begrudgingly stomped into the other room and came out with several plates. She set a few of them, then picked one up and twisted it around in her hands.

"You know, Luke, one day you'll—"

Suddenly, Laura screamed and dropped the plate. It smashed to pieces on the ground below.

There, at the window just behind where Luke sat, was a figure. A man with a gun. Just moments away from breaking in.

Chapter Thirty-two

ROBBERS AND RIFLES

The bandit bashed in the window with the butt of his shotgun, showering Luke in shards of glass. The boy yelped and leaped out of his seat, shaking the glass off him. He barely got to where Laura was, and she barely dragged him around the corner, when the gunman blasted apart the kitchen table.

"Handcart Sally!" the man shouted. "Get out here and get yours!"

There was no response. He cocked the gun forcefully.

"Don't make me tear up the house, Sally. Or tear up those kids."

He blasted a hole in the wall to the kitchen, and saw Sally diving to the floor. He reloaded and strolled on up. On the other side, Sally and the kids saw the bandit's eye peering through the opening.

"Boo!" he said.

Sally fired a plate at the hole, and they ran. The outlaw cocked the gun and blasted two new openings, tearing up the furniture and porcelain on the other side. He sauntered into the kitchen, spotting Sally's leg as they fled into the next room. He heard the cocking of a rifle from there.

"Now, that's more like it, Sally. Show me what you're made of!"

He marched towards the door. Sally yanked a lever on the other side, which armed a net trap in the frame. The bandit walked right into it, scrambling with the net until he toppled to the ground.

Sally knocked him out with the butt of her rifle, and the trio tied him up on one of the kitchen chairs. Luke stood watch with the rifle. When the bandit came to, he was all grins and no guns, but that didn't mean he had no ammunition. He had his mouth, after all.

"What's for dinner?" the bandit asked, before he cackled and coughed, and spit up something frightful.

"You, if you ain't lucky," Sally said.

"Oh, you eat men now as well as bury 'em, eh?"

"Is that what this is about? My past?"

"You ain't got a past, Handcart Sally. You got a present that goes back years, and keeps on goin'."

"I'm done with those days," Sally protested. "You one of Blood Johnson's lot? Thought you all disbanded. Thought we were done with everything."

"We'll be done with everything when you're done and gone. Ho, Sally, you can even tell us where to bury ya!"

"I'll be tellin' it to your grave soon enough."

"Make it big enough for all o' us, Sally. And make sure I can cosy up to that lass o' yours. Laura, is it? Yeah, we know all about you playin' happy family up here. 'Bout time we reminded you that you don't ever get to leave the gangs, Sally. Not without a bullet or a blade."

"Who sent you?" Sally asked.

"Who didn't? You worked up enough enemies over the years. Why, you might even rival the Coilhunter himself! And don't think he'll protect you. He's off fightin' this war o' ours. It ain't just a distraction, o' course, but it does a mighty fine job o' that. Oh, we're crossin' off names left, right, and centre. You know what they say about us. You've been marked by the Black Hand. Once you're marked, you're dead."

"So, this goes back to the mines," Sally noted.

"You used to make a pretty penny from those, didn't ya? Shaved off a little from the top too, so I heard. Don't think we didn't notice. Don't think Blood Johnson didn't know, either. He had a soft spot for you, but not us."

"The only soft spot Blood Johnson had was the one between his legs."

"Ohoh, he'd have had you by the rafters for that, Sally. Or he'd have had your sister between *her* legs. Don't think that demon amulet you got her makes her safe. Not from us."

"Not from the real demons, you mean."

The bandit cackled. "You've got wit, I'll give ya that. Pity we'll have to carve you up."

"You're not the first man to threaten me."

"But I'll be the last, Sally. I'll be the last."

"You'll be nothin'. You're already nothin'."

"Ho, I'll make a name for myself killin' you. Maybe they'll call me the Sally Slayer. Or the Handcart Killer. Maybe your Coilhunter friend will pin my poster up on his wall."

"You're crazy."

"We're all crazy in the Wild North, Sally. Especially the Coilhunter. You see, you have to be mad to march up here and live in this God-forsaken land. He forsook it for a reason. It's cursed land, this. Heard someone say the Anganda did the cursin'."

"No," Sally said. "It was cursed by you. By all o' ya. With your crime."

"Ohoh, she's a righteous one!" the bandit said to the kids, nodding his head at Sally. "You're a criminal too, Sally. Just because the Coilhunter took a shine to you doesn't mean anything's changed. There was still a poster for ya. Still got one myself back at the hideout. I'm sure Blood Johnson still has one too."

Sally shook her head and turned away. She wasn't sure what to do with him. She could let him go, but no doubt more of them would come. She wasn't even sure if more weren't already coming. Or she could kill him and bury him out in the yard. Like the good old days. Blood Johnson'd be proud.

While she was deliberating, she didn't see the bandit worming his way out of the bonds. He jumped up and grabbed Laura, wrapping his arm around her. He choked her with one hand, and kept the gun in his other pointed right at her head. Luke had lowered his rifle earlier and wasn't ready for this. As he tried to raise it again, the bandit eyed him with fire.

"Back away, boy, or I blow your sister's brains out. Right all over the floor!"

Luke stood there, shaking. In his mind, he already saw the bandit pull the trigger, the swiftly-cut cry, and the explosion of blood on the furniture. In his mind, he saw again the moment he pulled the trigger on his own father.

"*Please*," Laura sobbed. "Please just let us go."

"Let *them* go," Sally urged. "You can take me. You can kill me."

"Oh, we'll take ya alright. We'll kill ya alright!"

Luke raised his hand slowly, pointing his rifle at the man, straight at his exposed torso, which was just the right height for the boy. The gun felt heavy in his hands. The death of his father felt heavy too. But maybe this one would be different. Maybe it would be lighter now.

Chapter Thirty-three

NOT SO SHY

"No, Luke," Sally whispered urgently.

The bandit sniggered. "You ain't got the—"

But Luke fired faster than the man could speak. Perhaps he meant to say *guts*, and he might've wanted to pick a different word, because Luke's shot had the man's guts spilling out all over the ranch floor.

Laura's scream deafened the man's cry and grunt, and she leapt away from the splatter with limbs shaking more than Luke's were before. "You could've killed me!" she yelled. "You could've!"

"I saved you!" Luke shouted back. "He was gonna kill you. I saved you good!"

Laura covered her mouth, then moved her shaking hand away in horror as she saw a splotch of blood on it. Some stayed squeamish in the Wild North all their lives, but for most, it changed them. It made them look at the red and shrug, thinking: *at least it's not mine.*

Sally fired a handkerchief at Laura, having had a bit too much experience of the liquid red herself. Nothing that a bit of scrubbing couldn't clean up, after all.

"Block up the windows," she said. "There'll be

more of 'em."

Laura shook her head at the notion, but Sally cast a rifle at her before she'd fully dabbed the blood.

"We don't have time to dawdle," Sally said, "not if we want to live."

Luke was already nailing wooden panels across the broken window, though he left just enough space to poke a pistol through. Not for the enemy, of course. This'd be his bunker. He'd had dreams about fights just like it. The bad men came. And he had to kill them, one by one. You could've called it a nightmare, but for the folk of the Wild North, it was just daily life.

Sally and Laura barricaded the door, pushing a cupboard in front of it, and then the sofa.

"What about the back?" Laura asked.

"I'll get that in a moment," Sally said. "You get the side windows."

Laura pushed the remaining furniture up to the other windows, while Luke opened a large chest that was stored behind the sofa. He loaded guns by the dozen and piled them in the centre. They heard a sudden crash from the kitchen, followed by a shotgun blast, and then the dragging of the kitchen table up to the back door.

"I'm fine!" Sally shouted out. "That's another one. Don't let 'em get inside. Take 'em out, Laura! Take 'em out, Luke!"

Laura aimed out a hole in the wall and fired, but missed her shot. Her nerves were frayed. She reloaded and took out the advancing bandit just inches from the front door. Luke took out several others with one of the rifles he stacked nearby, never missing. He cleared the front of the house, then shifted to the side when he heard Sally yelling that more were coming.

"I can't see 'em!" he cried. "I need to go out."

"Don't go out!" Sally shouted.

"Don't be crazy, Luke," Laura said, as she took out another bandit.

"I can't get 'em though," Luke protested. "I can get 'em better outside."

"They can get *you* better outside too."

Luke blasted a few more, but bullets were starting to rain on the house from the side they couldn't reach. Laura screamed as one bullet pierced the wooden walls and struck her square in the shoulder.

"Stay down," Luke said, as he grabbed a four-barrel shotgun, one of the Coilhunter's designs. He dragged the barricades away from the front door, unlocked it, and strolled outside while cocking the gun. He walked around the left side, where several bandits were blasting the walls.

The shotgun boomed, killing the first. He cocked again, and the spent shell sprang away.

Bang. The second bandit tumbled. *Click click.* Luke was already on the third.

Luke took them out one by one, reloading with the speed of a sharpshooter. He'd practised a lot over the past year. He had to, what with all the bandits around those parts, not to mention the wildlife. There was a time when you would've called him Gun-shy Luke. Well, he wasn't so shy anymore.

Chapter Thirty-four

OVERRUN

When Luke came back inside, Sally grabbed him by the shoulders and shook him.

"That was an awful risky thing you did there, Luke!"

"I had to do somethin'!"

"You didn't have to do that. They're killers, Luke. You're just a boy."

"I'm a man now," he protested. "And I'm a killer now too."

See, it didn't matter how old you were. In the Wild North, you were born into bloodshed. You inherited the grudges of the gangs. You married into murder. And you gave birth to the next generation of outlaws. It was the cycle of life. Well, the cycle of death, at least.

"There's more of 'em!" Laura screamed. She pointed to the northern wall, which wasn't quite as bashed up as the others. That house was made to withstand a storm of sand, not a storm of men.

Luke was about to go outside again, but Sally grabbed his arm.

"You'll have to kill me first if you think you're goin' back out there."

Luke grumbled, but took up sentry duty on the northern wall, pointing his rifle through the cracks. He could seem them coming, dozens of them. He'd fought off bandits before, but this was different. These weren't just robbers and rapists. These were here to get Sally Hays no matter what. And Luke was there to stop them.

He gunned down the first wave, while Sally and Laura reloaded their rifles. Laura struggled with her shoulder wound, but she blasted that gun all the same.

The bodies mounted. From a distance, they kind of looked like sandbags piled on top of each other. Not that the desert needed any more sand. Not that the Wild North needed any more bodies either.

Then the final echoes of the gunshots died down, and everything was silent for a moment. They watched and waited for more, but it seemed it was over. They let out their first collective sighs of relief.

And that was when the Three Wheels Alliance came.

Chapter Thirty-five

THREE WHEELS, TWO ENGINES

The bikers came by their dozen, and they came in little gangs of their own. You see, the Three Wheels Alliance was made up of many different biker clans, all riding under one banner. They'd allied to each other, and then they'd allied to the Silent Sickles and the Black Hand Gang.

Most of the bikers rode hyper-hogs, motorcycles with three wheels and one hell of a chassis. Those wheels were all in a row, unlike the motorised tricycles or motorbikes with sidecars that some of the gangs used. And the wheels were thick, with giant tyres designed for the desert.

The rumble and thrum of the engines made the walls shake. A picture frame fell down, and the glass smashed. Behind those shards was a black-and-white photograph of Sally's deceased parents, obtained from old Five-pence Tully and her roaming dark chamber. She glanced at it now on the ground. It almost beckoned, as if to say: come join us, love. Come on up above. Or, well maybe, come on down below.

"Come out, Sally!" one voice roared. It belonged to Two-engine Ted, head of the Yellow Serpents, the most powerful of the united biker clans, and the one that came up with the alliance. He was a beast of a man, his muscles bulging through his shirt and leather jacket, his yellow mohawk being the only bit of hair on his head. Ted had brawn, sure, but he had brains also. That was the meaning behind the name. He used both engines of the mind, not just one. He'd seen his clan starting to lose power, so instead of just fighting more, he went for peace. Now they were as big as any of the non-biker gangs.

Sally didn't come out, and that didn't surprise them. That's when a different figure hopped off the bike behind Two-engine Ted. A familiar one.

"Oh, I'm sure she'll come out for this," Blood Johnson said.

Sally heard the voice and saw the figure through the gaps. Oh, he was missing a few of his gold teeth, sure, but that sickly smile could never be forgotten. His hair was a little more unkempt than normal, his beard wasn't trimmed quite as neat, and he'd aged quite a bit since she last saw him. You see, the Coilhunter had done his work on him, scaring him into exile. He'd sold everything, including some of his teeth, to get by. But now he was back. And he wanted blood.

"We mightn't make this," Sally whispered. She was never one to give up easy, but giving up now wouldn't be easy at all. She wasn't even sure they'd give her a quick death. They'd probably make her watch them to kill the kids first.

The engines revved. That was the equivalent of the twitch of fingers as they hovered over hips. They were the pre-battle sounds, the drum-roll before the clatter of gunfire. It was about to go down, and some were going to go down with it.

And then, folk turned to see a new arrival. There, in the distance, stood a silhouette: a tall, thin figure, with a broad hat, coat flowing, and scarf billowing. There, in the distance, stood Porridge, rifle in hand.

Chapter Thirty-six

THAT MULTI-COLOURED CAVALRY

Porridge was decked out as gaudily as ever, with mismatching boots, bell-bottom trousers patterned with multi-coloured stars, a half-unbuttoned black and white striped shirt, a torn and patched denim coat, and a cowboy hat with a pink silk rim. Even his gun was flashy, painted with yellow polka dots. If he was going to go out, he'd go out with style.

He advanced, taking out one biker who tried to shoot through the barricaded windows. Another biker turned to him, but he went down quick too. Porridge wasn't known for his marksmanship, but if you spent as much time with the Coilhunter as he had, you tended to pick up a thing or two. Porridge, known for scavenging, picked up a lot.

"Oh!" Porridge cried. "I feel like such a *man*!"

He kept going, taking out another. The burn of day was behind him, so he didn't have to squint to see his targets. The sun made a monster of his shadow, stretching it down to the front of the house.

"Oh!" he screamed with each and every blast of his rifle. "Oh, will you just lie there, pumpkin," he told one of the dead bikers. "Oh! Don't get up now."

He marched on. Well, maybe *march* wasn't the right word. He half-stumbled in those boots of his. You might've even thought one was just slightly shorter than the other. After all, comfort and utility was one thing. Style was quite another.

"I'm getting rather good at this!" Then he yelped as a biker drew close, before he blasted the man right off his vehicle. "Oh! Shoo! Shoo!"

He continued on, gunning down another of them. "Oh, plum, you'll thank me in the afterlife."

He looked brave at first, taking out one here and another there, reloading at he went. But as he drew closer to the ranch, he started into a trot, and then a full-on dash, screaming.

"Let me in! Oh!" he cried as he bashed his hand on the front door. "It's me! It's *meee!*"

The door swung open and Porridge fell flat on his face. Sally locked it behind as Laura and Luke helped Porridge to his feet.

"Oh, thank you, precious! Oh, thank you, plum! I was sure I was done for if I stayed out there any longer. Oh! And look what they did to my coat!" He held up his left elbow, where there was a splatter of blood from one of the bikers. "Dreadful! Just dreadful!"

"Boy am I glad to see you here," Sally said. "I presume Nox is out there clearin' up the rest."

"Why, no, peach," Porridge replied. "No, Nox isn't with me at all."

"Where is he then?"

"Oh! Bless my spinning cogs! I have no idea."

"But we need 'im," Laura said.

"I know, blueberry. Oh, I know!"

And boy did he know. He'd gunned down a few on his way there, but he saw plenty more driving up from the distance. There was four of them now, but that just meant more targets to kill.

Chapter Thirty-seven

HELL IN A HANDBASKET

Porridge paced to and fro restlessly. He'd come to their rescue, in a way, but it didn't take long before he felt like they might be coming to his.

"Why were you out here?" Sally asked.

"I was just passing through," Porridge explained. "Looking for my usual valuables. Oh! And thank the Heavens I found you!"

"I'm just glad you weren't off helpin' the Resistance."

"Oh, it's all gone to hell in a handbasket down South!" Porridge said.

"It doesn't seem much better up here," Sally replied.

"Don't remind me, peach. Don't remind me! Oh!"

But he needed no reminder. The thrums of the engines outside did plenty of that.

"Maybe we can barricade ourselves inside," Sally said, "like we did before."

"They have fire!" Luke shouted. He pointed out to where several bikers were lighting torches. It was clear as hell what they'd use them on. That ranch never looked so flammable before. Oh, it'd be hell in a handbasket alright, if the basket was their house.

If the Coilhunter had been there, he would have had a shiver in his soul. It was the fire that got his family before. Maybe it'd be the fire that got this new one too.

"Oh, if they set this place ablaze, we're done for! Oh!" Porridge shrieked.

"We'll have to fight outside," Luke said.

This time, Sally didn't object. It beat burning. At least out there, they had a chance. It wasn't a great chance, but it was still a chance all the same.

"Come on out here!" Blood Johnson roared. "Or we'll smoke ya out!"

The bikers lit the porch on fire to prove the point.

"We have to face 'em," Sally said.

They looked at each other, silent. Everyone knew it. Everyone knew this wasn't going to end well. Sally led them out, through the halo of fire, to where Two-engine Ted and Blood Johnson were waiting.

"Well, now," Blood Johnson said. "It's been a while, Sally."

"Not long enough," Sally replied.

"You thought you got rid o' me, huh?"

"Yeah, I saw you run with your tail between your legs."

"You cost me a lot, Sally. I'm gonna cost ya more."

Sally looked to Porridge and then the kids. The four of them stood back to back, ready to fight one final fight, as the bikers circled around them, and made that circle smaller all the time, intimidating them with the rev of their engines. This was it. They were done for.

And then, on the horizon, appeared a familiar

silhouette. A monowheel.

Chapter Thirty-eight

THE WAR ON WHEELS

The Coilhunter's appearance in the distance offered enough of a distraction. Some of the bikers broke from the circle to face him, while the others still stared off at the approaching figure, hearing the rev of his engine, and feeling now a little intimidation of their own.

Sally stared at Porridge with that look of *let's do this* in her eyes. He looked back more worryingly, perhaps because he really knew what she meant. *Let's do this without weapons. Let's do this without guns.* She glanced at Luke and Laura too. They also understood.

Sally leaped at one of the bikers, knocking him from his back. Porridge, Luke and Laura did the same, each from their own sides. Laura didn't so much as knock her biker down as end up on the back of his bike, half hugging him and half clawing at him. Luke ended up blasted backwards to the ground from the exhaust and spray of dust. And Porridge … well, Porridge caught his scarf in the wheel of one of the motorcycles and was dragged along, screaming, behind it.

* * *

Nox approached, and he pulled a four-barrel shotgun from a slot on the side of his monowheel. He blasted one of the tyres of an approaching biker, sending that vehicle spinning. He zig-zagged between the others, blasting at their tyres as well. When he was done with those shells, he smacked the gun off the face of the biker who rode up next to him, and then pulled another shotgun from the other side.

The bikers fired at the monowheel, but he zoomed out of the way. Some of them were forced to park to get a better shot, but that just made them easier targets for the Coilhunter. Others drew up on either side of him and tried to pin him, but he yanked a lever on the monowheel, which sent spinning blades out on either side, which tore through the tyres of his attackers.

The only biker who seemed to be able to keep up with Nox was Two-engine Ted, who followed the trail he left in the sand. They snaked their way through, guns blazing, until Ted was close enough to ram the monowheel from behind. The force of the knock sent Nox's vehicle spinning, and he fell from the seat, and the wheel came down on top of him. Luckily for him it was empty inside. The monowheel collapsed around him, sending dust spraying into the air.

He was quick on the draw though, blasting at the tyres and engine of Ted's bike as he passed. He puckered that vehicle like he meant to pucker Ted. And for the bikers, shooting up their bike was worse. They might've gone to war if you hung those bikes up by their wires instead of their families.

Ted's engine sparked from the Coilhunter's

gunshots, and Ted lost control. You see, he might've had two engines in his name, but his bike only had the one. His bike rebelled and drove him straight into a dune. Before he had a chance to get off, it toppled over right on top of him, pinning him in place. Now, those bikers wanted to be buried with their bikes, sure enough. But they wanted to be dead first. Well, let's just say the Coilhunter would be most obliging.

The others continued their struggle on foot, chasing or being chased, gunning or being gunned. Laura was cast off the back of the bike she hung onto, earning a few more bruises for her collection. Luke threw stones at others, but got hit with a few in the backfire, adding to his own.

Then there were enough fallen pistols and rifles to salvage, and enough remaining bikers to take them out with. Sally couldn't find Blood Johnson in the flurry, but she found plenty of others for her bullets. But she saved one just in case.

Porridge finally unfurled his scarf from his neck, and it went flailing into the path of another biker, catching in his wheel as well. Both bikes tugged it in different directions, caught in place, and then tumbled to the ground. By rights, the scarf should've torn, but Porridge didn't just buy or barter for any old thing. Fashion meant good fabric as well.

Nox hoisted his own vehicle up, which took some hoisting, and clambered back into the seat. He spun the wheel a little to let it dislodge the sand. Then he fired one of the front grapnel launchers, which had bigger claws than the ones he used on his arms, right into the torso of an approaching biker, throwing him from his bike. Nox grabbed a hold of the handle of the bike as it was about to pass him by, halting it in place.

"I'll keep this for now," he said, "'til ya learn some respect."

He drove off, slower this time, keeping one hand on the wheel of his vehicle, and the other on the handlebar of the bike beside him. He drove both of them, keeping them steady. The dislodged biker watched on as if he'd just witnessed a kidnapping. By the code of the clans, he had.

Nox reached Sally and the others and halted beside them with a skid. He tapped his hand off the chassis of the bike he'd captured.

"You okay?" he asked.

"For now." She nodded to west, where more bikers were emerging over the horizon. Nox nodded to the south, where a different shape appeared. A carrier landship.

"I hope that's your Resistance friends," Sally said.

"Not quite."

Sally clambered onto the motorbike, and Laura and Luke got on behind. Porridge climbed into the bounty box at the back of Nox's monowheel.

"Let's roll," Nox said.

The large, flattened carrier on landship treads trundled closer. It was about half the height of them, which made it harder to spot in the desert, but it was wide and deep.

"What is it?" Porridge asked.

"Backup."

"Oh, it'd better be an army, plum."

The Coilhunter smiled with his eyes. "It is."

The door on the carrier opened and a ramp extended. Nothing else happened for a moment. And then they came. One by one. Then a dozen at a time. Lots and lots of mechanical ducks.

Chapter Thirty-nine

THE BUTCHER OF THE BIKERS

Nox zoomed off to face the bikers, with a trail of toy ducks waddling behind him.

"Oh, how did you make so many, precious?" Porridge asked, as he clung on to the Coilhunter.

"I didn't. Oddcopper made most of these. I had 'im workin' on 'em for weeks."

"Well, plum, he certainly cooked up a lot."

Nox smiled beneath his mask. "Fresh from the oven."

"Oh, I'm glad I kept the Dandyman out of this," Porridge said. "If those bikers were smart, they would've kept their vehicles out too. Oh!"

Nox continued through the mass of approaching bikers, gunning down the bikes to save the riders. That was sacrilegious to them, of course, but hey, it saved their lives.

Yet there was one life he didn't mind taking. Two-engine Ted. You see, Ted wasn't just head of the Yellow Serpents and the Three Wheels Alliance. He was the ringleader of numerous gang rapes throughout the region. He was smart enough to get away with it for now, but even the smart ones got dumb every once in a while. Like now. Like facing Nox.

Two-engine Ted led a kind of cavalry charge at Nox, right down to the arrow formation. He might've thought that would've broken the Coilhunter, that it would've sent him turning. But he didn't know Nox. He only knew the rumours. And he hadn't listened closely enough.

"We're going to crash, parsnip! Oh!" Porridge cried.

"Yeah," Nox said, and he pushed harder on the accelerator.

There was a game some children played in the Wild North. They called it *chicken*. It could involve anything, but the goal was to see who'd chicken out first. Sometimes it was close. Sometimes it went right down to the wire. But someone always baulked. Someone always turned at the last second.

That look of determination in Two-engine Ted's eyes turned to terror, when he saw the Coilhunter wasn't turning. When he stared into the Coilhunter's eyes, he saw a different look, one that came with a message: *I'm gonna get ya, even if we all have to go up in flames.* For the Coilhunter, who'd faced the fire before, that was saying something.

But Ted was a bright fellow. A smart fellow. A fellow who wanted to live.

So, he turned his bike at the last moment, and the other bikers turned, but Nox fired his grapnels at them, and kept on going. He zoomed through the opening they just narrowly formed, halted suddenly, and yanked hard on a lever. Large metal prongs extended from the monowheel and shot into the ground, pinning it in place. But the motorbikes kept going in the other direction, until the grapnels tightened, and pulled them back with force. The bikers, including Two-engine Ted, were thrown off into the sand.

Nox climbed off and wandered over to where Ted was nursing what looked like a broken arm. You could repair a lot on your bike and your body, but not everything.

Nox fired two rounds into Ted's head, one on either side.

"There," Nox said. "A bullet for both engines."

Sally knew horses, but she knew motorbikes as well. You had to when you were embroiled in gang warfare. She'd put those days behind her, but she hadn't lost the muscle memory. Why, it was like riding a bike.

A group of bikers hounded her, hemming her in from the side. Blood Johnson trailed from the back. He'd let the others do the dirty work, but he'd get his payout all the same. Nothing had changed with him, except maybe now he was a little more desperate than before.

Sally zipped across the sand. The bike gained airtime as it zoomed over the top of a dune, and came down hard on the packed sands beneath. Some parts there were more earth than grain, but those tyres tore through them all the same.

The other bikers followed, clipping the chassis every now and then with a token shot. That bothered the bikers more than it bothered Sally and the kids. They didn't want to damage that bike, even if it was stolen. You see, Sally had a hostage after all.

One biker seemed faster than the others. He came up close to Sally, trailing her, and then came up on the left side, before falling back again. And there he was once more, level with her on the right. He was toying with her, showing he couldn't just match her speed, but pass it. Then he rushed ahead and turned right into her path, forcing her to slow a little more. He was cutting off her path. The others would be back soon enough to hem her in, to cage and kill her.

So, Sally rammed the biker. The trio shook from the force. Now, if you rammed a biker's hog, you might as well've smacked them in the face. It wasn't just an insult. It was an invitation for a smack in return.

The biker grabbed a rifle from his back, but he only got his fingers on the handle before Sally turned a little, sped ahead, then turned sharply into his bike, sending him skidding out of control. His bike didn't just topple, but somersaulted down the dunes, crushing him beneath it.

Sally pursued the fallen biker and yanked the rifle from his back. She tossed it to the kids behind her.

"Gimme it!" Luke cried, as he tussled with Laura. "I'm a better shot than you."

"You didn't used to be," Laura said. "And besides, I have an injury."

"It doesn't matter who shoots," Sally said. "Just one o' ya do it!"

So Luke fired, while Laura grasped him by the shirt to stop him falling off. There were half a dozen bikers approaching from the right, but the next time Sally glanced that way, it was just half a dozen bikes rolling to a stop.

"On the left!" Laura cried.

Luke turned and took out half a dozen there too. You see, he didn't mind hitting the bikers or the bike.

The ducks piled into the battlefield. Some bikers froze on the spot, while others turned and fled. Some of them had a working engine in the head after all. But there was one duck in particular that stood out. You might've known him. You might've wished you didn't.

"Get your blinders on," Nox said, as he pulled on a pair of blackout goggles.

Porridge took out a pair of his own, which were a bright yellow, edged with purple. Nox signalled to Sally, who had goggles for her and the kids. When you knew Nox long enough, you kept them handy.

The duck turned its head, watching the figures approaching.

"Quack!"

The blast was blinding. It sent bikers into each other. It sent some tumbling down dunes. It sent others toppling over on the spot. Men bawled and clawed at their eyeballs. You see, it didn't just blind you. That white light burned too.

Nox parked his monowheel and got off. He appeared as just a voice to some, or a vague figure to others. But one by one, he was the man who knocked them out with his rifle. You were saved the bullet then, but that might've only been temporary. You see, he might've saved it for later.

There was one man, however, who didn't deserve saving.

"Blood Johnson," the Coilhunter said, and he

smirked. "Ain't that a sight for sore eyes."

Blood Johnson squirmed on the spot. Oh, he'd been there before, blinded by the light. He saw the shimmering silhouette of the Coilhunter, a phantom from another world, a creature from a criminal's nightmare.

"Do you wanna do the honours?" Nox asked Sally, as she drew up beside him.

Sally looked at Blood Johnson, not just now with disgust, but pity. This man had hounded her for years, getting her into bigger debts so he could own her. He was just a loan shark, but the Coilhunter was just a lone wolf. He'd let him off with a warning last time. As he'd shown before, he didn't warn you twice.

"Now that I see 'im," Sally said. "I'm not sure I do."

"That's fine with me," Nox said, before he unloaded a bullet in Blood Johnson's head. See, he'd already spent his pity. Men like Blood Johnson didn't have any pity for the Northfolk, for Handcart Sally, or for the Coilhunter himself. No, they only had self-pity, blaming the world for their troubles, excusing their behaviour because of past hurts. Some of them had it bad, sure enough, but that didn't mean they had to be bad themselves. That was a choice. And when you chose it, you chose the Coilhunter as your enemy, as your destiny.

The battlefield was littered with bodies and bikes. The wounded and the captured were watched by the toy ducks, some of which stood still, staring ominously at their captives, while others waddled back and forth along their sentry routes.

Yeah, Nox had brought an army. What those criminals didn't know was that only a handful of them did anything special, anything scary. The rest of them did nothing at all.

WHEN THE DUST SETTLES

It was all quiet on the northern front, as the saying goes. It was only quiet, because so many were dead. You see, war makes a lot of noise, but it makes a lot of silence too. Dead men don't talk.

"Oh, reunited at last!" Porridge cried, piercing the quiet air.

"I don't think it was that long ago I saw you," Nox replied.

"Oh, too long, pumpkin. Too long! Besides, I've got some new fashion to show you." Porridge tipped his hat. "Inspired by you, you know. Oh, isn't it something?"

"It's somethin' alright."

"Oh, I looked the part, precious. And I acted it too. Oh, I was cocking my gun here, there, and everywhere! Oh!"

"What made you come out here?" Nox asked.

"Oh, my ripened raspberries, Sally asked the same thing. You're made for each other, you know."

"Only because I was the hunter and she was the hunted once."

"Oh, now don't be coy, Nox. You know I mean more than that, don't you?"

"You didn't answer my question," Nox said.

"And you, little dandy, evaded mine. I was just scouting the area in the Dandyman, looking for some good scrap to add to my collection."

"To scavenge," Nox said, remembering his own monowheel was once in Porridge's sights.

"Well, waste not, want not," Porridge said. "Oh, and I saw all these bikers on the move, plum, and I just *had* to see where they were going. When I saw they were approaching Sally's ranch, I knew I had to don my cowboy hat and grab my rifle. Oh!"

"It was lucky you were here," Nox said.

"Oh, I have a tendency to be in just the right place at the right time."

"Or the wrong place at the wrong time."

"Depends how you look at it, peach. I've gotten dear old dandy Rommond out of a pickle or two. Oh, and Nox, I think I've gotten you out of some as well."

"And into some also," Nox rasped.

"Well, you can't win them all."

"Where are the others?"

"Sally's tending to Laura's wounds inside." He nodded to the house, where the last embers of the porch burned low. Sally had managed to get the flames out in time before they engulfed the whole building. "She could be a doctor, you know."

"She could be anything she wants."

"Oh, honey, don't say that as if you don't want her to be yours."

"Where's Luke?" Nox asked.

"Hmm. I think he's calming the horses. Oh yes! There he is. He's a gentle one, isn't he?"

"Yeah," Nox said, "though he wasn't gentle with those guns."

"Boys and their toys. Oh!" Porridge fanned himself. "Which reminds me, plum. What're you going to do with all those toy ducks? I wouldn't mind one myself, you know. A little memento for what we've been through and all."

Nox scooped up one that was waddling past. "There," he said, plopping it into Porridge's hands. "It's just a decoy anyway."

"And the rest of them? What's the plan for those?"

"They're gonna pay a little visit to the other gang members who've survived this war."

Chapter Fourty-one

JUST PAPER AND CHARCOAL

Nox strolled over to where Luke was combing the horses. They'd calmed a lot since the battle. You'd think they would've been scared of the Coilhunter, but just like his friend Chance Oakley, he was good to animals. He was even good to the mechanical ones.

"Luke," Nox said.

The boy didn't respond. He kept on brushing.

"I hope those gunshots didn't blast your ears, boy."

"What d'ya want?" Luke asked.

"I … I just wanted to check that you're okay."

"I'm okay," Luke said. "The horses aren't."

"They look fine to me." Nox didn't say what he thought next: *I'm not so sure about you.*

The air was quiet. One of the horses whinnied.

"You like horses, huh?" Nox asked.

Again, Luke didn't respond.

"I know a man who likes horses too. They say you can often judge a man by how they treat animals."

"You can judge 'em by how they treat people too," Luke said, with a hint of anger behind his voice.

"Is somethin' wrong, kid?"

Luke kept on his silent brushing.

"You know, I'm sorry I didn't stay."

"No, you're not," Luke said. "Just like mama and papa weren't. No one stays and no one's sorry."

"Sally stayed," Nox said.

"Only 'cause you made her."

"I didn't make her do anything. She wanted a family. She wanted you."

Luke turned, and there were tears in his eyes. "And what about you, Nox? What did you want?"

"It's not what I want, boy. It's what I can't have. It's what I have to do."

"Sally said that about you too."

"It's true, though, Luke. Don't think it doesn't hurt me too."

"I thought you couldn't be hurt," Luke said. "I thought you were just a phantom, a shadow, a symbol."

Nox paused and let his breath out slowly. "Underneath all that, underneath the mask ... I'm a man too."

"I waited for you," Luke whimpered. "I thought you'd come."

Nox let out another of those stifled sighs. "I'm here now."

"Well, you don't have to be. We've done fine without you. I'm the man of the house now. I can defend us all. We don't need you!"

Nox was about to reply, but the words didn't seem fitting. He couldn't offer any reassurances, and he certainly couldn't offer any promises he knew he couldn't keep. More than anything, he couldn't say what was buried not just behind the mask, but behind his heart. Those never-spoken words: *Maybe I need you.*

He stood there for a moment, watching the boy groom the horse and move on to the next one. He thought maybe the kid would say something else, but he didn't. He thought maybe now wasn't the right time. Maybe things had to settle some more. Besides, he still had to talk to Sally and Laura inside.

He turned to leave and spotted Luke's notebook on a nearby rock. He picked it up before the boy could see him. Last time he'd seen it, it was full of marvellous drawings. Even one drawn lovingly of him.

"What's this?" Nox asked, as he flicked through the drawings and halted on one that seemed a little disturbing.

"It's nothin'," Luke said as he peered over and caught a glimpse of the one Nox was staring at.

"It ain't nothin', or it wouldn't be here."

"It's just a drawin'."

"What is it? Do you see this when you sleep?" He knew the bad dreams all too well. They were bad already, but they got worse after each and every kill. You see, no matter when or where you got rid of the bodies, you never got rid of them fully at night.

"It's just a drawin'!" Luke shouted.

"Quieten down, boy, and answer my question."

"I don't want to think 'bout it," Luke said with a pout.

"If you're drawin' it, you're thinkin' about it."

"It doesn't work like that. It's how I get 'em out."

"But what is it?"

"Just a figure."

"Tell me, Luke."

Luke shook his head. He seemed frightened. "I don't wanna, Nox."

"It'll help if you do."

"I don't think it will. I think it'll make it worse."

"Who's the figure, Luke? Why did you draw it like this?"

"Please don't make me say it, Nox."

"Who's the figure?"

Luke's lip trembled. "It's … it's … you."

Nox turned the notebook around. He saw the resemblance now. It had his hat and coat, his mask, his guns. It was him alright, but a twisted, warped version of him, all jagged, with eyes like a demon, and parts of him merged with machine. A mere glance sent shivers down his spine, his human spine. But, as Luke said, it was just a drawing. Just paper and charcoal. And yet Nox couldn't help shake that horrible feeling that it was so much more.

Chapter Forty-two

CATCHIN' UP

When the Coilhunter entered the house, Laura ran to him and hugged him.

"It's been so long!" she said. "What've you been up to? We've been fendin' off bandits here for months. Never thought it'd get this bad though. Did you see what they did to my arm? Sally got the bullet out and stitched it up. Look!"

Nox inspected the wound. "Wear it like a badge," he rasped, before tapping the multi-coloured sheriff's badge on his chest.

"Oh, I will," Laura said. "But I'd rather they just left us alone out here."

"Hopefully they will now. Most of 'em are dead." Nox paused. "Where's Sally?"

"She's in there, washin' up."

"Give me a minute with her, will ya?"

"Sure. I'll go check on Luke."

"He might need a minute too. Or more than a minute."

"He's just bein' moody. He'll come 'round like he always does."

"I hope so."

"Trust me, he will."

Nox stood in the doorway of the kitchen, watching Sally mopping up. There was a lot of blood everywhere.

"You never did visit," Sally said.

"I was—"

"Don't say you were busy."

Nox paused. "Okay."

"You should've visited."

"I just wanted 'em to be safe."

"There's more to life than bein' safe, Nox. What about bein' loved?"

"You've gotta first start with bein' safe."

Sally sighed. "Well, we weren't safe, were we?"

Folk said the only way to not win or lose is to get out of the game. That's what Handcart Sally had tried to do. She'd cashed in and cashed out, ending her association with the gangs of her past. But that was the thing about the Wild North. It didn't let you leave. It kept playing the game against you, and it had its cards stacked and its dice loaded. It had the dynamite stacked and the guns loaded too.

"Thank you for comin' though," Sally said. "Not sure we woulda made it otherwise."

"I'm only here for a while," Nox said.

"I know."

"I wish I could stay longer."

"I know."

They stood there in the silence for a moment. Sally mopped the same patch of floor.

"Did you see what he drew?" Nox asked.

"Don't pay no heed to that, Nathaniel. It's just the imaginations of a child."

"I thought he was a man now."

"In his mind, perhaps, but he's still just ten years old. He hasn't much changed since you met him."

"I think he has."

"Oh, he can shoot now, sure. But he's still the same old Luke."

"Are you sure about that?"

"Don't you worry about him, Nox. He's just a little troubled is all. Couldn't blame 'im after what he went through. And we're all a little troubled in the Wild North. Sure, wasn't I once?"

"Yeah, and you resorted to crime as a result."

"And I found my way again. Besides, you're more than a little troubled too, y'know."

"I ain't no criminal."

"No, you're the law," Sally teased.

"Keep an eye on 'im, will ya?"

"Of course. I keep two eyes on 'em both. That's what you asked me to do. Well ..."

"Well, what?"

"You asked me to raise 'em. You gave me a family."

"I'm glad you think so."

"Just a pity I can't give ya one back."

"I have a family," Nox said.

"You've got ghosts, Nox. We've all got 'em, sure, but you're the one who haunts yourself."

"Let's not have this conversation again."

"Why not? You say Luke's changed, but what about you? Don't you think maybe change is good? At least he's processin' his demons, gettin' 'em out on the page. What do you do?"

Nox approached the door and held up his pistol.

"I process 'em with this."

RIGHT IN A ROW

In some parts of the Wild North, the night was the worst. If it wasn't the cold that'd get you, it was the nightcrawlers, the part-spider, part-scorpion, part-God-knows-what. And if it wasn't those, it was the gangs that thrived in the dark, the Night Slavers or the Black Silk Collective. And if they didn't wrap their hands around your sleeping throat, then maybe it was something else. Maybe it was the Sandsweeper. Or maybe something worse.

"What's that?" Fingers Franklin said as he roused from sleep. He was a thief by name and a thief by trade. He'd worked with all the big names in the past, robbing banks and robbing trains. Some said he'd rob himself one day out of boredom.

"It's just the wind, ya fool," Hammerhead Helen replied. You could guess where she got that name, but few men guessed anything about her before she slammed her skull against theirs. They said she had a daytime temper, because she slept pretty soundly at night.

"The wind don't make no noises like that."

"Come back to bed, Frankie."

"No, I'm on edge now. This war's gettin' outta

hand. Do ya think they sent someone?"

"If they did, kill 'em quick and come back to bed, will ya?"

Then something like a nightmare crept into the room. It was small and clung to the ground. Its shadow stretched over Fingers Franklin, as if to reach out to grab him. It halted a few metres into the room, still in darkness, with the moonlight casting a glow around its grim silhouette.

Yeah, a thing of nightmares. At least for the criminals of the Wild North. There, in the darkness, stood a toy duck.

"H-h-helen."

"Hmm?" she mumbled.

"Helen!"

She sat up and barely opened her eyes enough to see the silhouettes of a dozen toy ducks in the room before her.

"W-w-what do we do?" Fingers Franklin stuttered.

"I don't know! Reason with 'em! Bargain with 'em!"

"I don't know how to do that!"

"This was 'cause you robbed that bank."

"I've robbed lots of banks!"

"I always said you shouldn't do it. We had enough coils. It's greed is what that is."

"This isn't the time for a debate."

"Now we're gonna die to ducks, all for some stinkin' coils we didn't need."

"Will ya help me or what?"

"It's fittin', actually. Didn't you rob a toy store

before this too?"

"That wasn't me. That was Tricks Taylor."

"Coulda sworn it was you. Where'd you get the music box, huh?"

"Well, I got it from Taylor, but I wasn't involved in the robbery."

"Likely story, that. Do ya think the ducks will believe ya? Do ya think the Coilhunter will?"

All across the Wild North, the rooms of criminals flooded with toy ducks, freezing most of them in their tracks. What they didn't know was that only a handful of them were capable of what the so-called Mr. Quacky could do. The rest were simple toy ducks. They say what you didn't know couldn't hurt you. But fear could hurt. Fear could kill. Fear had them all shaking in their bedsheets.

Then fear spoke, and it spoke with the voice of Nox.

"Criminals of the Wild North," he croaked. The voice came loud through one of the ducks, which had a radio made into its frame. "It's time to end this war. You started it with six, but I'm endin' it with hundreds. Move a muscle and I'll sling you up like you hung those kids. Your leaders are dead or dyin'. Your friends are dead or dyin'. Your families are dead or dyin'. This feud ends tonight. It's up to you whether it ends with your lives."

BURYIN' THE HATCHET

Nox arranged a truce between the warring gangs, bringing them to the table for the first time in years. Frank Five-eyes was there. James "Ironking" Dalton was there. Iron-chair Ivy was there. Jimmy Tombthief was there. Those were the surviving leaders. The other two were new: Guzzler Garret, the new chief of the Good Gullet Gang, and Amanda Oakley, the new head of the Three Wheels Alliance.

It was something else seeing them around the same table, former rivals, now ready to ink a deal to end the bloodshed, and save themselves from the Coilhunter's list.

"This is where we bury the hatchet," Nox said.

"Proper lawman, that," Guzzler Garret said, nodding to Nox.

"As if," Dalton replied, perching up in his seat. Oh, he had one just like Iron-chair Ivy now, though not quite as good. "It was Lawless Lyle who had you all 'round the table before, with a gun to your heads. This ain't any different."

"Oh, it's different," Nox said, as he circled the room. There were a whole lot of toy ducks perched along the walls, surrounding everyone. "There ain't a gun in sight." And there wasn't. Nox'd made that a rule before the truce began.

Amanda Oakley scoffed. "Who needs guns when you've got gadgets?"

Nox eyed her up and down. He couldn't quite remember the name Chance Oakley told him before, but it might've been that. Amanda. Oakley's wife. Well, former wife. The one who abandoned him, just like his friends did, when his gold mine went from diamond to dust after the Iron Empire changed the currency to iron. Nox might've grilled her on that if it weren't for the fact that it'd likely upset the peace deal. The other stuff, the personal stuff, would have to wait.

"I've read through this," Jimmy Tombthief said, holding up the terms of the accord, "and I think it's a mighty fine document."

"Didn't think ya could read," Amanda Oakley said. She didn't have a fancy name like the others. She didn't like them. No, she had Chance Oakley's name. That bothered Nox more.

Frank Five-eyes was silent. He'd already lost most of his forces, and already had his signature on the page. But he never looked at it. He just stared at Jimmy Tombthief with gun barrels for eyes.

"You break this deal," Nox said, "and war between you will be the least of your troubles. This is law we're talkin' about. This is bindin'. And there's a penalty for anyone who breaks it."

Nox knew they'd break it eventually, some sooner than others. It'd be small things at first. Petty crimes. A little robbery here and there. A bit of encroachment on enemy territory. Of course, it only took a little thing to start a war.

Iron-chair Ivy signed her name. "We're agreed." Behind Ivy stood Harmony and Double Dice Henry. Nox could've sworn those were wedding bands on their fingers.

Amanda Oakley was the last to sign. Nox hoped that wasn't an omen. Some folk said the last to sign it was the first to break it. Of course, most folk only ever signed their will.

Nox held up the document. "I'm gonna hold you to this."

They nodded. All of them.

Peace for our time.

Not all men wanted peace, though. Nox had learned that many times by now, and kept on learning. Some couldn't let go of their grudges. Some couldn't let go of their hate. Oh, you could sign your name alright, but if you didn't also sign it on your heart, it meant nothing at all.

Chapter Forty-five

TOMBTHIEF

The deal was done, and the ganglords went home. Jimmy Tombthief's home was out of the way, out near Loggersridge, where Nox came from. Out of the way was good when it came to the Wild North. Out of the way of the fire. Out of the way of the gunfire.

"I spoke with Saul," Jimmy's wife, Mariah, said.

"And?"

"He assured us protection from the Deadmakers."

"But what about the Coilhunter?"

"No one gets protection from him."

"That Handcart Sally does. Heard he foiled the attack on her ranch."

"Well, Saul has a plan to take 'im out."

"He always has a plan. He has a hundred plans. What about the execution?" Jimmy Tombthief smiled. "And I mean that both ways, honey. Both ways."

"He said *one of—*"

"*One of these days*, yeah. I heard it before. What about today, huh? We've been on a lucky streak here, layin' low while the other gangs tore each other to shreds. We'll be the stronger one when everything settles, before that truce ends. And this alliance with the Deadmakers will make all the difference. We've gotta make the most of it before our luck runs out."

"We just need to give it time."

Jimmy Tombthief grumbled. "And what did you give Saul, huh? I hope it was just gold and iron."

"Don't you trust me?"

"I trust no one, honey, and you know that. I've lost too many to the desert, and I've lost the rest to trust."

"Well, they trusted you too, you know," Mariah said. "The Good Gullet Gang an' all."

"They trusted me to take out Frank's kid. Even the odds a little. Cull the curs. I did my bit. We did our bit. The alliance only means somethin' until it doesn't. It's a means to an end, and the end is comin' quick. It's high time the Authentic Antiques Assembly has a more prominent place up here. The Deadmakers will help a lot with that."

Mariah shook her head. She'd heard a lot of that before. The end was coming alright, and it'd come for many of them already.

"Let me put Jennifer to bed," she said.

"She's outside," Jimmy replied. "Playin' on the tree, I suspect."

"It's gettin' dark," Mariah said. "I better call her in."

"Leave her. You coop her up in here too much already."

"I coop her up in here 'cause I'm afraid of all the enemies you make."

"The Deadmakers will change that, honey. I promise."

"They better, and it better not be another curse

with that name."

"It's a curse to their enemies, Mariah. This deal with Saul makes 'em our friends."

Mariah gave him a look that showed she wasn't quite certain about that. She knew all about the friends he made. The Good Gullet Gang and the Broken Bones Gang were among them. They were all fair-weather friendships, and the thing about the Wild North you learned quick was that there was no fair weather. Even when the sun was beaming, it was there to burn. Even when the wind was still, it was so the stalkers of nature and men could hear and hunt you.

Mariah went to the door, opened it, and called for her daughter. "Time to come in, Jennifer."

"I'll be in in a minute," Jennifer shouted back.

"Five minutes tops," Mariah said. "It's too dark to be out now."

"Ten minutes."

"I said five. I mean five." Unlike her husband's broken promises and broken alliances, she really did mean it. She kept her word. It was perhaps the only reason she still stayed with him. *Till Death Do Us Part* weren't just words to her. They were a contract. You didn't just sign it with God. You signed it with Death.

Mariah stood there watching for a moment, taking some pride in her daughter's adventurous side, and some comfort in the fact that she could still see her silhouette perched on the old oak tree. Then she went back inside and closed the door.

And there, just to the side, in the deepest and darkest shadows, was a figure. There, in the dark, was

Frank Five-eyes.

Chapter Forty-six

THE TREE OF LIFE

There was a tree on Jimmy Tombthief's estate. You mightn't have thought much of that, but where he lived, the land was parched, so a tree growing there was something else. It was a symbol of life, and it was a symbol of power, because only the rich could afford to water a tree when so many in the Wild North could barely afford to water their own throats, let alone their bodies.

They called that old oak the Tree of Life. It was about the only lucky thing in Jimmy Tombthief's life. He watered it daily, religiously. He fed that soil just as much as he fed his own daughter. Well, Mariah's daughter. It was a kind of child to him too. Hell, some said you could rob his gold and he'd forgive you more than if you cut down that tree. That was saying something, because Jimmy Tombthief had a lot of gold, and a lot of other ancient riches, which now only had value to the few.

Little Jennifer would climb that tree and sit there for hours, watching the wild horses that sometimes travelled by from tribal lands. There were no wild horses there that night. Something had spooked them. Spooked them good.

She heard the crack of a branch in the darkness.

"Five more minutes, momma," she asked. She glanced back, but the door was closed. Her mom wasn't there, arms crossed, counting down the seconds.

Maybe the sound was from the horses after all. Maybe they were out there in the darkness. It kind of seemed like something was. She couldn't quite see it, but she could sense it.

"Is that you, Blackmane?" That was her name for the stallion she figured was the leader of the herd. He was a majestic beast. Some day she thought she'd right a horse just like him.

She climbed down to get a better look. The night was thick and daunting. The darkness seemed to smother everything. Her eyes had gotten pretty used to it, but this time it seemed darker than normal. She'd overheard her father talk about a plot by the Night Slavers to make every night just like that, and every day too. But that was just a story. Like the ones they said about the Coilhunter.

She stepped out into the blackness. She couldn't tell what she was stepping on, except for memory. She wondered how the horses did it, and why they were out there so late. She knew her mother wondered why she was out there so late as well.

Another step. Another pool of shadow swallowed her feet. It was so hard to see. But Blackmane was a dark horse. He wouldn't be seen easy in the shade.

Another crack. No, that wasn't from her feet. She hadn't stepped on anything but ground. It was from behind her, back near the tree.

She turned back. The tree was different. What was that new shape? It looked like rope hanging from one of the branches.

"Are you playin' games?" she asked. She imagined that Blackmane liked to play games. He was wild, but maybe he had a lasso to hold him in place. Maybe that was where he'd anchor. Maybe he'd let her ride him after all.

"Momma said—"

A man came out from the shadows behind her. He seized her, silencing her with one hand. He pinned her arms with his other. Her eyes were wide with terror, wide enough to stare up at Frank Five-eyes' face above. But she didn't know it. And she'd never be able to speak his name.

Frank's massive hand didn't just cover her mouth. It cupped her jaw. He moved her head this way and that to get a better look at her.

"So young," he said. "Just like Toby."

The girl whimpered, but didn't scream.

"So brave," Frank said. "Just like Toby."

He hoisted her up and brought her to the tree. The silhouette of the noose was clearer than ever.

"How we pay for the crimes of our fathers," Frank said, as he wrapped the rope around the girl's neck. "Find a better papa in your next life, girl."

The Wild North wasn't known for its trees or forests. It wasn't known for the rough bark or the tough branches. But it was known for its hangings and its killings. It was known for the slain elderly and the youthful dead. It was known for moments like this.

Frank pulled the rope tight.

Five more minutes. Pity you couldn't ask that from life.

Chapter Forty-seven

ONE FOR EACH OF YOU

When news got out of little Jennifer's death, there were threats of renewed war in the wastes. It'd only been days since the peace deal was signed. Nox'd promised to enforce it, like he enforced the other laws the lawless didn't sign. You put your name down or he'd put you down instead.

Frank Five-eyes was missing for days now. He hadn't returned to the Farmlands, and hadn't been seen at his ranch near Millroad either. It didn't take a genius to know that he was behind it. The fact that he ran just added to the crime. Nox didn't even need a poster.

It took the better part of a week to track him down. He'd been sighted at the caverns just north of Millroad. Seemed he wanted to die close to home after all. You see, you could run all you wanted in the Wild North, but sooner or later the Coilhunter'd find you. Sooner for Frank.

It was a thick night when he got him, just like the night he took that little girl's life. Nox parked the monowheel nearby. The light from Frank's campfire carved out their silhouettes.

"It's over," Nox said, as he came up behind him.

Frank shook his head viciously. "It's never over."

"Let me end it for ya then."

Frank turned and emptied his revolver at where Nox had been.

"You missed," Nox said, and his voice seemed to come from the other side. When Frank turned, it seemed like the Coilhunter's figure was there as well. He glanced back, still seeing the silhouette of Nox in the shadows where he'd been before.

"How many of you are there?" Frank cried, incredulous.

"One for each of you," Nox said, as another Coilhunter seemed to appear in the darkness ahead.

Frank pulled back, pointing his second gun left, then right, then straight ahead. His hand bobbed from one to another as his eyes peeled in horror. He turned to run, but another two figures stood behind him. He would've needed those five eyes to watch them all.

"Do you know what haunts my sleep?" the Coilhunter croaked. It seemed to come from behind Frank, so he turned and fired a single shot. The figure shifted a little, but didn't fall.

"Do you know what keeps me up at night?" the Sandsweeper drawled. It seemed to come from the right, so Frank fired there too. The silhouette was as unmoving as ever.

"Do you know what frightens me in the dark of dream?" the Masked Menace crooned. It seemed to come from the left, so Frank blasted the phantom on that side as well. Still it stood, arms ready for the draw.

"It's the thought of just how many of you there are," Nox said, his voice flowing around the circle. Frank tried to follow it with gunfire. "It's the thought that no matter how many I kill or bury, there'll always be more. There'll never be a big enough grave."

"I give up!" Frank shouted. "Show yourself. Stop this torture!"

Nox showed himself first with a bullet, which struck Frank in the leg and brought him to the ground. Nox strolled out from the shadows, passing one of the spring-loaded scarecrow figures donned in clothes just like him. He snatched the cowboy hat as he passed and placed it on.

"More games," Frank said. "More tricks!"

"You like to play games in the dark when it suits ya," Nox said, "and you like to bend and break the rules. Well, welcome to a game I like to call the Lawless and the Law. Do you wanna know who won?"

"It ain't fair, Nox. They're the ones who started this feud."

"And you kept it goin'. Year after year. Death after death."

"But they started it."

"And I finished it," Nox said. "Just a pity you wouldn't listen. Just a pity the only way you could bury the hatchet is in the body of another. You know what they say about an eye for an eye."

"I'm Frank Five-eyes!" the man cried in defiance.

"And look how blind you are."

"I could see the end," Frank said. "Just a few more of 'em. A few more of those monsters and I'd be done!"

"But that's the thing. You said that before. Just one more name. Just one more kill. Then you'll be done. Then it'll be over. But that's the thing about vengeance. It's never over. It's never equal. It's never even. You can't balance things with vengeance. You can only balance it with justice."

"This *was* justice," Frank protested.

"There was nothin' just about it. Your goons tore up the Burg, slaughtered the townsfolk. Your goons blew up the mines, killed the maimed. Your goons attacked the ranch. And you, well, you hung that child up all by your lonesome. You know that ain't right. You know that ain't just. And the moment you did it, you knew I'd hunt you down."

"Well, you caught me, Nox. Now what?"

Nox fired even before he finished the words. Frank grunted and groaned. There was still a little life in him, but it was fading fast. Just like his gang was fading. Maybe the war would die with the ones who fought.

"I didn't want to kill you, you know," Nox said. "I know that loss. I know that pain."

"Then we're the same," Frank coughed, "you and I."

"No, we're not the same. I took my pain and tried to make somethin' of it, tried to make this forsaken land into somethin' better. You wanted revenge for yourself, and hell, I get that."

"And what did you want, Nox? Huh?"

"I wanted justice for all."

Frank's voice faded, but not before he coughed up one last remark. "And did ya get it?"

The ganglord passed on, so there was no real reason to respond. But that's not why Nox was silent. Sometimes the criminals passed like they lived, just a number on a lawman's sheet. Every so often, however, they said something in their death throes that did a little bit of soul-haunting.

And did ya get it?

Nox's voice was as grim as ever. "Not yet."

Chapter Forty-eight

BETTER TERMS

Nox returned to the Farmlands in the dead of night. You did a lot of things in the dead of night, because the dead of day would far too often live up to its name. You didn't need a spotlight to out you then. That big old ball of fire in the sky'd spotlight you just fine.

But Nox escaped the watchful eyes of the Farmlands' guards, and the waiting barrels of their guns. He stalked the walls, sending those artillery gunners to sleep with a well-timed butterfly capsule.

Some of the children were still working the fields. Maybe it was a punishment, or maybe the Baron just had them all doing different shifts. Either way, it was clear they were tired, and clear they weren't being treated well by the guards.

As Nox darted through the shadows, he spotted children sleeping in haystacks to the side. Others slept on the ground. Some huddled together, because there weren't enough blankets for them all. They were all born after the Harvest, the time the Iron Empire came to that world, and supposedly conquered the birth channels with their infernal magic. Or so the stories went. But when you saw them there, all those so-called "demon" children, shivering in the night air, the only monsters you thought of were the ones who made them slaves.

Nox found the Baron's quarters after some polite interrogation of a nearby guard. Oh, he showed bravado at first. But by the time Nox was done with him, he was shivering too.

The Baron's room was lavish. His bed was packed high with a thick mattress and many blankets, not to mention silk sheets. He was snoring loudly. Some folk thought to ask the criminals: *How do you sleep at night?* Well, by the looks of it, just fine. But not that night. The Baron was about to have a very restless sleep.

Nox sat cross-legged on the cushioned bench at the end of the bed, and took his steel-plated guitar from his back. He waited for a moment for the Baron to shift in his sleep. You see, you had to know you had them in their nightmares too.

Nox played his tune. The criminals knew it. The conmen knew it. The gangs played it to their new recruits, so they knew what to listen for. Some played it for the children to get them to go to bed. In real beds. Not the straw stacks or the cold ground. The twang of that tune was haunting. It spoke of sorrow. It spoke of anger. It had all the Coilhunter's history in just a few strums of the strings. It told you he was coming.

And now, as the Baron awoke in a fit of sweat, it told him he was here.

That Baron had shown bravado too, just like his guard, back when the Coilhunter was there before.

But not this time. This time he was alone in his room with the Masked Menace. This time the Baron screamed.

"Let's save that scream for later," Nox rasped. "Or maybe, if you're lucky, let's save your life as well."

"Don't hurt me," the Baron pleaded. He knew Nox had gotten Frank Five-eyes. He knew he'd get them all in time.

"Whether I hurt ya or not depends on you."

"Oh, please."

"Now, I like those manners. Let's hope by the time I'm through with you, you say *thank ya, sir* as well."

The Baron's teeth chattered. He looked periodically to the door, undoubtedly hoping to hear his guards passing by outside.

"It's late," Nox said. "I put 'em all to sleep. Look how late it is, Baron. Go check your bedtime clock."

The Baron turned to his bedside table, where his alarm clock used to be, and recoiled in horror at the sight of the mechanical duck perched there, staring at him with those blank eyes. Those painted-on eyes.

"You know who else should be sleepin'? Those kids you have workin' outside."

"They prefer the night shift," the Baron lied.

"And do you?" Nox asked. "Do you like this night shift of ours?"

"What can I do? What do you want?"

"Better terms is what I want. Better terms for the kids."

"I can give a little," the Baron said.

"You can give a lot." Nox took one pistol out

slowly and rested it on the waist of his guitar, pointing it dead at the Baron.

"What do you want? Anything!"

"Beds. You give 'im beds. Not those haystacks in the barns. Real beds. Real linen. You make 'em warm, y'hear?"

"Yes! Beds!"

"And food. Real food. Not that slop you serve. You give 'im oats. You give 'im beans. And meat once a week."

"I can't afford that!"

"You can't afford not to. You give 'im a share of that good old God-given produce you talked about, or I give you back to God."

"Okay! Okay!" the Baron shrieked. "Food. I'll give 'em real food."

"And rest. Proper rest. Time to play. Time to read. You get 'im books from the Mugs and Pages Inn. Good books. The stuff the Regime outlaws."

"Fine, Nox. I'll get 'im books."

"And the time off."

"And the time off."

"And a bath. Once a week. You pay up extra to the Dew Distributors to get ya the water."

"Hell, Nox, you'll bleed me dry!"

"Oh, I'll bleed you dry alright, if you don't make this the damn finest place for these kids to live and work."

"Okay, Nox. I'll do it. Just … just let me live."

"Let them live, and I mean really *live*, and I'll let you live too."

"I already said I would!" the Baron whimpered.

"Good," Nox said, as he stood up and put his pistol and guitar away. "Oh, and let this be a contract," he added. "You know what I do to those who break 'em."

"Of course. A verbal contract. I give you my word!"

"No, you see, I've gotta ink that paper." The Coilhunter strolled over to the visitor book on the stand nearby and grabbed the quill as if he were a quillslinger. He came back to the Baron and prodded the pen into his arm until it drew blood. The Baron yelped, but didn't budge. "Now," Nox said. "This time I'll sign my name. Consider it our contract. And let it be a reminder in case you're ever tempted to lapse."

Nox went back to the visitor book and dabbed the blood down on the page. He used a name he hadn't heard often, though he was sure he'd forgotten some of the monikers the Northfolk gave him over the years. As the blood formed the letters, it felt it rather apt.

Redranger.

He let the quill clatter off the ground as he departed. "Don't make me come back and sign another."

Chapter Forty-nine

THAT TEMPORARY PEACE

There was one more place on the Coilhunter's list he knew he had to visit before he could take a few days for himself back in his workshop, where he'd work on the next round of toys, the next round of gadgets.

They called it the Bounty Booth, a ramshackle hut on the south-eastern edge of the Wild North, bordering Iron Empire territory. They used that place to keep things in check, so they wouldn't ever have to worry about fighting a war up north as well. Some said they used Nox for that too, but he didn't mind. The law was the law, no matter who you were.

Nox entered the Bounty Booth, spotting Hardwell at the counter across the way. He was an Iron Empire man, down to the uniform. They obeyed orders, and he was ordered to keep that booth stocked with posters on the walls and coils behind the counter.

"Haven't seen you in a while," Hardwell said.

"I've been busy."

"So I heard. Didn't seem you needed any Wanted posters at all."

"No," Nox said, "but I still remember the faces."

He strolled past the wall that was overrun with

posters, many on top of each other, like the graffiti of the waiting dead. He yanked a handful of them down as he passed and piled them on Hardwell's counter.

"You'll find the bodies on that desert lawn o' yours. Well, parts of 'em, anyway."

"You can't cash in after the fact," Hardwell said.

"I can," Nox replied, "and you're gonna pay up. You don't make the rules here. I do."

"But this is an Iron Empire establishment."

"This," Nox said, gesturing around him, "is the Wild North. This is my territory."

"Some might say you're just as bad as them," Hardwell grumbled, as he placed several bags of coils on the counter. "Robbing me blind."

"No, I make sure folk can see. Your Regime want to keep the mess of the Wild North from spillin' out into their lands. Well, they gotta pay for the privilege. And if they fall—"

"The Iron Empire will never fall."

"That's what the gangs here said, and the Iron Empire is just a bigger gang."

"I hope that's not a threat."

"Call it an eventuality."

"No one can tell the future, Nox."

"Maybe not, but I can tell the present, and I can tell ya what I plan to do about it. One by one, I'll clean out these parts. And when I'm done, when there's a little bit o' law and order here, I'll clean out the rest. And here, let me do some extra cleanin'." He plucked another half dozen posters from the wall and rolled them up in his pockets. "Some for the road," he added.

"Well, just remember that I'm an ally," Hardwell

said.

Nox smiled with his eyes. "We're just associates by circumstance, Hardwell. I'm allied to somethin' else, somethin' bigger. I'm allied to life. Allied to law."

"Well, life doesn't always go on the same," Hardwell said.

"Then we'll adapt."

"And law doesn't either."

Nox tipped his hat. "Then we'll adapt to that too."

You see, life doesn't go on the same—but it does go on. As Nox vanished into the shadows, he knew that in some ways life would change in the Wild North, but for every toppled gang, there'd be another to take its place. He'd taken on six, and won. Maybe six more would fill the void. Well, there was always another day. Another night. Another six bullets in his gun.

About the Author

Dean F. Wilson was born in Dublin, Ireland in 1987. He started writing at age 11, and has since become a *USA Today* and *Wall Street Journal* Bestselling Author.

He is the author of the *Children of Telm* epic fantasy trilogy, the *Great Iron War* steampunk series, the *Coilhunter Chronicles* science-fiction western series, the *Hibernian Hollows* urban fantasy series, and the *Infinite Stars* space opera series.

Dean previously worked as a journalist, primarily in the field of technology. He has written for *TechEye*, *Thinq*, *V3*, *VR-Zone*, *ITProPortal*, *TechRadar Pro*, and *The Inquirer*.

www.deanfwilson.com